The Oregon Project

The Oregon Project

by

Natasha Roit

Tapestry Press
Arlington, Texas

Tapestry Press
2000 E. Lamar
Suite 600
Arlington, TX 76006

Printed in the U.S.A.

10 09 08 07 06   1 2 3 4 5

Library of Congress Cataloging-in-Publication Data

Roit, Natasha, 1960-
  The Oregon project / by Natasha Roit.
    p. cm.
  Summary: "A murder mystery in which a con man, two candidates for the
office of District Attorney, and the Chinese mob all get involved in murder"--Provided by publisher.
  ISBN 1-930819-48-X (pbk. : alk. paper)
  1. Public prosecutors--Fiction. 2. Political candidates--Fiction. 3. Swin-
dlers and swindling--Fiction. 4. Triads (Gangs)--Fiction. 5. Oregon--Fiction.
I. Title.
  PS3618.O535O74 2006
  813'.6--dc22

                                    2006010065

Cover by David Sims

Book design and layout by
D. & F. Scott Publishing, Inc.
N. Richland Hills, Texas

Dedications

To Becky

When this book was at its infancy, you came into my life with your unmatched kindness, human insight, and uncompromising strength. You made me see that "the true test of a person's character is not in falling down but in standing up" is not just an old adage but a defining moment in one's life. You showed me the way out of the perpetual labyrinth of work and into passion for life and everything it has to offer. Thank you for standing in the fire with me.

To Judi

We met under unbelievably difficult circumstances in your life. If there were ever a person who could claim the right to be bitter, it was you. And yet, over the past decade that I have been privileged to know you and call you my friend, you have handled yourself with grace and strength. You have supported me and all I did and you stepped into a role in my life with your maternal wisdom and life passion that is uniquely you.

CHAPTER

The Alley

On any given night, this alley was permeated with a brew of dumpster trash and drug-filled urine. Its filth was matched only by its darkness and the scent of gut wrenching fear emitted by anyone who happened to turn into it by accident or, as in this case, was brought here against his will.

He stopped feeling his hands somewhere midtown. Luckily, the rope cut off circulation and relieved him of the pain. Now, he knew, it was only a matter of time—his time. The stench of the alley hit as soon as he was dragged out of the back of the black sedan. There were three of them, but he could only feel two now, one on each arm, pushing him further and further into the abyss of this strange location, which would soon become his final resting place. Where was the third? Did he stay with the car? Was he the one holding the gun, and would put the bullet in his head? Did any of it really matter?

He tried to push his mind to think about his life or hoped that it would flash before him. There was his wife, his two children. Why would anyone want to visualize their families in their minds before dying? And if you did, did you also feel the emotions, the pain, the guilt, the joy, the sorrow, a sense of satisfaction, and the taste of disgust that accompanied one's life with his family. Or did it all, at those final moments, mesh into some storybook picture that assisted the dying and fooled them right into the next world. And if you feel nothing, what's the relevance of the visual? What's the point of your mind's eye? What's done is done.

He tried to pray, not because he thought it would do any good, but because, somewhere, in the recesses of his mind, he knew that he should. But to what God? The one that brought him to this end? The one he defied by getting himself here? And what does one say to his maker, here, reduced to the lowest denominator of human existence, caught up in the ease of destruction of that which God created. But then, it can't hurt to pray. That is if he could.

In the final analysis, neither his mind's eye roaming through his past nor his anomalous attempt at prayer could overcome the feeling of pure fear—not of the unknown, mind you, but worse, of what he knew would simply be pure extinction. Literally, a dead end, not unlike the cold concrete wall that ended this atrocious alley.

He had nothing more to offer them, and they stopped asking an hour ago. What he could give them, he did. He gave them names, locations, and what he knew about his deliveries. There was no loyalty to the others. He did the jobs because he was lazy and this was an easy way to make a living. He was no more than a messenger—one envelope for delivery and one for him with cash. That's all. No office to go to, no tie to wear, no boss whose crap he would have to take. He knew the risks, but they seemed worth taking and, frankly, unreal.

Now, a decision was made, and it was irreversible. The only question was how hard they would hurt him, and how long it would last. After all, the message was no longer for him, but for those who would find him, see his body, see his autopsy photos, read about him in the papers. He was now no more than an instrument, a method to convey what would be done, a token of the way things were or must be.

On some level—some strange level—it was surprisingly comforting. After all, he had no more decisions to make—ever. No more wondering when and how his end would come. Those poor living slobs. They were the unlucky ones. Living in the dark about the future. Living in fear of the unknown. Some working hard for an old age that would never come. Some living with a foreshortened sense of the future, unprepared for long but unfulfilled lives. Not him. All he had to do was give in to what was inevitable. He did.

Each crevice of the filthy slimy wall seemed to find its way into the pores of his face. He could not see the blood dripping down his skinned cheek, but he could feel the warmth of it. It would not be long now.

But suddenly, with an understandable yet futile sense of urgency and hope, he began to fight. It was less heroic and more instinctive. Not unlike a bug covered by a shadow of a shoe one hundred times its size, with the outcome all but certain, but with a minute possibility of escape. Why not?

He squirmed and moaned and kicked. Again and again. He could feel that he finally connected. He got one of them in the shin, and heard the concomitant swearing and felt another blow. He got the other one with the back of his head and simultaneously saw a blinding light. It was his head playing tricks on him, he was sure. How ironic. He would die from his own actions. Instead of successfully escaping, he would pass out and not even feel the barrel of the gun pointed at the back of his head. Nor would he hear the squeezing of the trigger. When the bullet would penetrate his brain, he would die quickly and quietly. His lifeless body would be found in this pit of degradation. This dark alley in Chinatown.

Or maybe he was already dead. Maybe this was the light, this blinding light, you were supposed to see when you died. When you met God.

The Dinosaur

At the district attorney's office on the thirty-fifth floor of the stifling downtown Los Angeles tower, Grant Bellinger was sitting at his mahogany desk reading up on the latest polls. It's not that he was uninformed of their content, or had not already barked his commands in response. He simply enjoyed defeat as much as victory, as long as he predicted it and could be proclaimed to have been right. In his fifty-two years on this planet, he learned that, in the great scheme of life, only two things were important, being right and leaving no doubt about it. As such, he was now making his record for whatever the outcome.

"That punk is catching up to me," he cursed to his campaign manager, Timothy Newsome, Jr. "Have you seen the latest polls? Landau is within ten points, and the elections are still a month away. Three terms in this freaking office, hundreds of criminals convicted, and it's still not enough for these ignoramuses."

"Well, frankly, despite your conviction record, which, I must say is impressive," Newsome was trying to appease his boss, "people are afraid to live in this city. You've been in office a long time, and they are more afraid today than they were when you were first elected. It has nothing to do with you—granted—but the electorate is unforgiving. They want a scapegoat, and Landau is doing a good job making you one. Besides, he is young, tough, and smart. The Berardo conviction got a lot of press, and Landau's face was plastered all over the media. The public doesn't quickly forget putting away a mafia boss."

"That punk worked for me when he tried that case. I wiped his nose during that trial." Bellinger snorted.

"I know that, but the public remembers his name as the prosecutor."

"Public." Bellinger griped with disgust. "Same pool of stupid two-legged vacuums who serve on juries 'cause they are too dumb to get out of jury duty. It's bullshit that I have to rely on them to figure out who is the better D.A." Bellinger paused for effect.

"This is my swan song," he continued, "I am not going out except on my terms, with a big retirement party and a gold watch. And it's your job to make that happen."

"I am doing my best, Uncle Grant." Newsome said.

"That's crap, little Timmy and you know it. Now listen. Your father may have been my best friend, but this favor cup is about to run dry. Besides, if you served in the navy under your father's command the way he wanted you to, he would have kicked your ass a long time ago—made you get down and give him twenty or something equally traumatic for your wimpy composition."

"Maybe," Newsome thought to himself, "and if you were under his command, you would have been court-martialed a long time ago, before a crowded gallery, with me in the front row." But now was not the time. Bellinger controlled the strings, and Newsome needed the job, and would swallow the bad taste.

Besides, he was quite at ease, so to speak, with the verbal abuse—not unlike children who are victims of domestic violence being drawn to abusers, Newsome was most comfortable in this environment. Your own skin, no matter how unhealthy, is still a better fit than a stranger's.

Indeed, Uncle Grant rather nicely filled that amorphous gap when Timothy Newsome, Sr., a highly decorated war hero, died. The substitution was rather natural. Bellinger was part of their lives since little Timmy could remember. And like his father, he demanded unflinching respect, whether or not he deserved it.

"Look, I think it's time we attacked Landau personally." Bellinger decided. "I knew all along that your advice about 'no negative campaigning' was wrong. I think we should dig and find something on him. He just comes off too squeaky clean."

"Don't you think this is risky?" Newsome asked. "Attacking someone who worked for you. I don't know. I think it can backfire. Besides, if we dig, he will dig. It could get ugly."

"See, that's your problem, in a nutshell, little Timmy. No guts. You know what your father said to me when you decided to pursue this line of work? I remember it like it was yesterday. He said, 'Perfect, like shit pushing up flowers, Timmy is going to stay below ground because he is a coward. My son chose to be shit.' And that's a quote, Timmy. Now, either do your job and get me elected, or tell me right now you don't have the balls to do it, and I will get someone else." Bellinger concluded.

❧

In a military courtroom in San Diego, California, a brash twenty-five-year-old JAG (judge advocate general), wearing his over-ironed uniform, was prosecuting a corporal who drove drunk and killed a civilian family. The defense argued that, although the drinking took place during leave, the corporal was amidst his superiors, also drinking, and felt compelled to participate. The JAG walked around the courtroom with ease, confidence, and an air of ownership normally reserved for older and much more experienced lawyers. He was in the middle of his closing argument.

"Even if you accept the argument that the defendant felt he had no choice but to drink with his superiors, an argument that clearly has no merit, he had an option to go back to barracks with his superiors, and he declined. At that moment in time, no matter what else you believe, he was on his own. He broke any chain of causation. He tore any string, ripped any connection. He alone chose to get into his vehicle. He alone chose to start the car. No one pressured him to do that. No one ordered him to turn that key. And no one, no one, but Corporal Jensen himself drove over the double yellow line, causing the head on collision, causing the death of three innocent people."

"That's going to be you," whispered Timothy Newsome, Sr. to his twelve-year-old son, sitting in the audience in that military courtroom and pointing to the young Grant Bellinger delivering the closing argument. "That's going to be you."

❧

"Is that going to be you? Is that going to be you? Newsome, are you listening to me?" Bellinger was addressing little Timmy in his office twenty-eight years later.

"Yeah. That's fine. I can do it." Newsome said quietly.

On that note, Bellinger swung his chair away from little Timmy and towards the window, dismissing his campaign manager like the dispensable servant that he was.

Palestine's

That evening, Tess Lowe was preparing for a showing at Palestine's on Sunset Boulevard. Her blond hair was tied in a bun, accentuating her soft white skin and high cheek bones. The teal silk pantsuit she was wearing outlined her tall narrow frame. At thirty-two, she was that perfect mixture of young, beautiful, and self-assured, glowing with the kind of self-knowledge and appreciation for herself that women simply do not have until they breach that third decade mark.

She was right, as usual. Wayne Anderson was making quite a stir, and she expected a good turnout for the display of his works and, hopefully, their sale. Before coming to Tess, Anderson had been turned down repeatedly by galleries. His art was too modern, some said, too wild, others lamented, or just plain weird, the rest determined. Not Tess. It was precisely this combination of reactions it drew from people that appealed to her. The works were a combination of paintings and sculptures, abstract and portraits, all in one piece, all meshed to draw and mesmerize.

As has become her practice, she tested the waters at The Gallery Restaurant, displaying two pieces only, strategically hung near the most desirable booths. Jim Pane, the proprietor of The Gallery, and Tess's mentor, would seat just the right clientele under her selections and surreptitiously solicit feedback. She came to Jim literally off the street—a cold call she made, intrigued by the unique nature of his restaurant. He agreed to work with her on consignment. She brought him the works of various artists. He displayed them.

In the case of Wayne Anderson, the response was overwhelmingly positive. After three pieces sold in a matter of weeks, Tess delivered the good news to her client and immediately prepared for a full showing.

Palestine's was a perfect spot. Not so big that the displays were dwarfed, but big enough that the importance of the demonstration was paramount. People were starting to pour into the gallery and browse. Some were good clients whom Tess invited personally, of course. Some were strangers solicited through a mass mailing and teased with a brochure.

They were all meandering now, staring at the art hanging on the walls and pretending to read into it a meaning well beyond what the artist intended. Anderson, wearing black slacks and a white silk shirt, was quietly chatting with another man and pointing to one of his works. A distinguished looking older couple was discussing another piece of art in the corner.

Tess's attention was drawn to a young man in a grey pin-striped suit, who had walked into Palestine's, but had not moved towards the art. He was tall, thin, with short dark hair. Based on his looks alone, he would have easily melted into the crowd. But, as with many things that draw queries without answers, he emitted charisma that belied his otherwise average appearance.

The man was downing his glass of champagne and had just called over a waiter carrying hors d'oeuvres. He stuffed a shrimp in his mouth and looked up to catch Tess staring at him. Her first reaction was to leave him alone, give him time and space to take in the inventory. There was nothing worse than walking into a store and being immediately bombarded by an over-anxious salesperson.

But the man was not moving. In fact, he was simply looking at her, as if he were stopped in his tracks by a "please wait to be seated" sign, and waited for the hostess to assist him. Tess, being that hostess for all intents and purposes, walked up to him and asked,

"Can I be of some assistance?"

"Some more champagne would be nice," the man answered. Tess flagged a waiter with a tray. She handed a filled glass to the young man and took one for herself.

"I am Tess Lowe. I represent this artist. Is there something in particular you were looking for?"

"Well, if I tell you the truth, do you promise not to kick me out?"

"You like it that much, Mr. . . ."

"Parks. Charlie Parks. Frankly, this stuff is not my cup of tea. Give me a picture of a meadow or, better yet, a self-portrait, and I am happy as a clam. But this stuff, what does one do with it, anyway?"

"Well, I would presume they hang it on their walls and enjoy it. Are you in the market for a particular type of art?"

"Yeah, the type that strikes my fancy. You know. I can't describe it, but I'll know it when I see it. Just like beautiful women." Charlie answered.

"Are you hustling me, Mr. Parks?" Tess asked.

"Yes, I am." Charlie answered with cocky confidence.

"Well, I'm afraid we don't give discounts for charm. And, in your case, that is certainly too bad." Tess gave her route answer to the less than inventive come-on, although she was unsure if she was more turned off or flattered.

"Why is that?" Charlie asked.

"Because I bet that you can charm your way into anything. By the way, you wouldn't happen to be selling real estate investments, would you?"

"Oh, you've heard about me, then."

"Jim Pane is a good friend of mine. He believed in me when no one else did. I owe him a lot. He's been like a father to me. And with that, he sometimes gets rather paternalistic."

"Mr. Pane is a smart businessman who can take care of himself. What about you?" Charlie asked taking another sip of champagne.

"So this is what your visit here is all about. You're looking for another investor. Well, you've come to the wrong place, Mr. Parks. I am not interested, and I don't mean to be rude, but I am working."

"No problem. Jim asked me to talk to you about the investment, but, frankly, I would rather take you to dinner."

"You have a better chance being struck by lightning on a sunny day." Tess answered instinctively. She got asked out often, and the process had long ago become more annoying than entertaining.

She learned that any glimmer of hope contained in her initial answer would be mistaken for interest, while direct blunt negative responses would catapult her immediately into the bitch category. She preferred the latter.

"Lunch then." Charlie pressed unabated.

"Not even coffee. Thank you, though, and, again, I don't mean to be rude, but I have business to attend to." Tess walked away and joined the Japanese tourist group arguing feverishly over something in the brochure.

Sauntering out of the gallery, Charlie made sure that he rewarded himself with another shrimp.

The Lion's Den

It was a warm Friday night. Charlie Parks turned on the interior light of his Jeep Cherokee in order to look once more at the map. He thought he was lost, but the map told him that he was on the right course. He turned right towards the entryway of a gated community, and drove up to the gate. A burly security guard leaned out of the booth and asked where Charlie was headed.

"George Stone's residence. I am expected."

"Oh, yes. The Stone party. Of course, sir. What is your name?"

"Charlie Parks."

The guard grabbed the list on a clipboard by the phone, located the name, crossed it off, and wrote out a pass slip. "Put this on your dash. When you drive in, go to the second street and turn left. It's the house at the end of the cul-de-sac. You'll see a lot of cars there. You can't miss it." The guard raised the gate arm.

Charlie marveled at the homes on both sides of the street. He had heard about Bel Air, and had a mental image of it, but he had never come here before. Some of his customers at Johnson Mercedes lived in Bel Air. He thought then, as he sold them their top-of-the-line cars, that, despite the different backgrounds or professions of these people, they had one thing in common. They were rich.

It mattered little how they got their wealth, or how long they had it, or even how long they would keep it. What mattered is that they have been there, to that coveted spot in the world reserved for the few—those who do not calculate before they buy, those who do not worry about qualifying for a loan, those who sign on the dotted line without much negotiation, even when they know that they have overpaid. Charlie was convinced that many knew they were paying too much and, in fact, liked it. It was that ability to condescend without saying a word. You think you got me. Fat chance. Ultimately, in the game of life, I got you many times over.

The homes were all large with immaculately manicured lawns and three car garages. The guard was right—you couldn't miss George Stone's house. There were probably fifty cars parked outside, none costing less than $40,000, Charlie was certain. There were at least two limousines and a valet standing in front of the house wearing a name tag that said, "Arturo, Prime Valet Service."

Charlie pulled up to Arturo and handed him the keys to the Jeep. He walked up the brick driveway outlined by custom Florentine path lights. The front door was unlocked, and Charlie opened it. The entryway was lined with Italian marble. Straight ahead was a Lucite staircase curving around and leading to the second story. Charlie could not quite tell if this house had a third floor. An elaborate crystal chandelier hung from the ceiling and dangled over the entryway, lighting up the staircase. To the right and the left, the house was filled with people and their endless chatter.

Charlie located George in the living room talking to a man who looked familiar, although Charlie knew he had never met him.

"Charlie," George Stone called to him. "I'm glad you could make it."

"Grant, I'd like you to meet my new business associate, Charlie Parks." The men shook hands and Charlie recognized the man from the TV commercials.

"Thank you for coming to my fund-raiser, Mr. Parks. We can use all the help we can get." Grant Bellinger returned to his conversation with George Stone. "Can you believe that he's taking credit for the Berardo conviction? I wiped his nose during the trial, that punk."

Charlie took a step back to allow the host and his guest of honor their semiprivate conversation. "You son of a bitch, George," Charlie thought as he continued to catch bits and pieces of Bellinger's rambling. "You're throwing a fucking fund-raiser for the very man who should throw your ass in jail. No wonder you've survived unscathed for fifteen years. I have a lot to learn from you." Charlie stepped in closer, and decided to start the learning process.

"How can we help, Mr. Bellinger. How can we help you defeat Mitchell Landau. This city needs an experienced district attorney like yourself. It doesn't need someone like Landau cutting his teeth on the job."

"You're a smart young man, Mr. . . . ."

"Parks." George helped his old friend.

"Mr. Parks. Well, like anything else, a campaign costs money. We need to keep playing our commercials, and getting the word out that I am tough on the criminals, and that I am the man, not Landau, who can keep this city together. I am certainly grateful to George for holding this fund-raiser. Anything we can do to raise funds to give them one hell of a fight in the next six weeks—that's what we need."

"Indeed," said Charlie. "I told George when he invited me to the fund-raiser that I was thrilled to contribute to such a worthy cause."

Timothy Newsome approached his boss a few minutes before, but did not dare interrupt the conversation. When it appeared that Bellinger was taking a breath, Newsome reminded him that he needed to refresh his memory on the speech for tonight, and that it may be a good idea for them to go to one of the empty rooms and practice. Bellinger reluctantly agreed and excused himself.

"You're a quick study." George told his protégé when they were left alone.

"Thanks for the compliment, George, but I don't appreciate your inviting me to the lion's den without warning. And by the way, it's a nice pad you've got here. Is it really yours or did you just wipe someone's name off the deed and put yours in instead?"

"Don't be a smart ass, Charlie. It's mine. It took time, patience, and perseverance to get here. But most importantly, it took brains. In our business, you have to learn to control your downside. Speaking of which, what's going on with The Oregon Project. I've sent out the first round of checks. Are you making any progress? Remember, you've got thirty days, and then we're pulling out—and it's not negotiable."

"Don't worry." Charlie said. "I'll have the rest of the money before that old fart Bellinger learns that his friend George is one of the people who should be behind bars in his commercials."

"Then you're a few years too late." George said staring straight into Charlie's eyes. "I suggest you leave a generous contribution to the old fart's campaign before you leave tonight. I know Mitchell Landau. He still believes in justice and the tooth fairy. We can't afford to let him get elected. He will dig deep to find a way to reassure the public that they made the right choice. Nothing would do that better than to go after someone whom Bellinger let slide because he got paid off."

"You?"

"Maybe."

"Would be a shame to lose all this." Charlie said swinging his head towards the chandelier.

"Yes. But it would be worse to lose your freedom."

Throughout his life, Charlie thought of what it would be like to be in prison. But like most young people who think they are invincible, he never thought of prison as a reality. He did now. Maybe it's because he finally had something to lose.

Although he was only thirty years old, Charlie had had his hand in a number of schemes, and had never been caught. He began his less than illustrious career at sixteen when he scalped concert tickets with his buddy, Mickey Dagwood. One weekend, they each made three hundred dollars, a fortune to a teenager. Mickey immediately spent his money on drugs. Charlie bought new clothes and a fake I.D. so he could get into the Sonata Night Club. He was unusually tall for his age, and, with his new adult looking garb and a fake I.D., getting into the coolest club on the West Side was a cinch. There, he met Joey Cancino, who introduced him to liquor, women, and other small time crooks.

Charlie worked for Joey until he turned twenty-two, at which time he reunited with Mickey to run a valet service. They called it "C & M Valet Service." They frequently joked that instead of their initials, "C" really stood for "crook" and "M" for "miscreant." Their seventh grade teacher, Mrs. Paulson, put the word "miscreant" on a quiz, and when Mickey objected that learning such words was a waste of time, Mrs. Paulson insisted that one day they would be glad that they had such an extensive vocabulary that would impress any prospective employer.

After taking temporary possession of the keys from the unsuspecting public, Charlie would take an impression of the car key and copy the address from the registration usually left in the glove compartment. He would hand the key and the address to Mickey who sold it to his connections. In the days that followed, the cars of those who enjoyed dinner at "Jimmy's" would disappear. Mickey's pals asked Charlie to copy the house keys of those who left them hanging on the same key chain while they dined. Charlie refused. He had his limits.

"Is there anything else we can do for Bellinger besides money?" Charlie asked George.

"Newsome is having Landau checked out. Until then, we write out checks, watch the polls, and pray. Come on, there's someone else I want you to meet. His name is Hsiao Tzu, which literally means 'little pig' in Chinese. He runs a chain of dry cleaners and Chinese laundries."

"Why do you want me to meet the little pig? You think now that I have more than one suit, I should have my own personal dry cleaners?"

"He doesn't clean my suits, Charlie," George said. "He launders my money."

CHAPTER

The Assistant D.A.

Mitchell Landau was in the middle of a preliminary hearing on a murder one case at the Criminal Courts Building. He was thirty-three years old and had always had political ambition. He frequently sought out cases that would get him the most press and took great care of his public image. But now that his every move was being watched as part of this heated campaign between him and Bellinger, he found the constant attention both invigorating and tiring. With the election only six weeks away, he was closing the gap in the polls, and he knew he could outlast his boss ("The Dinosaur" as he was called by the people at the district attorney's office).

He did not have much time to prepare for this hearing, but assigning it another A.D.A. (assistant district attorney) was bad politics. After all, if he did not have time to handle such a routine matter now because of an election, what would he be like with the added duties of a district attorney. He was sure that was why Jackson Boyd, his worthy opponent, refused to waive time for a speedy trial and pushed this hearing forward.

The Constitution guarantees every criminal the right to have his fate determined sooner rather than later, in a well-meaning attempt to free those who did not commit the crime. Ironically, it is usually the guilty who choose not to waive this right, hoping to prevent the prosecution from properly preparing for trial and from meeting that high burden of proof beyond a reasonable doubt. The innocent almost routinely waive timely trial in order to mount a proper defense to assure their ultimate release.

"Call your next witness, Mr. Landau," ordered Judge Betty Spencer, staring over her reading glasses.

"The prosecution calls Thelma Chow to the stand, Your Honor." Landau announced.

A middle-aged Chinese woman made her way to the stand. She was dressed conservatively, in a dark skirt and a sweater, and clutched her well worn purse with her left arm as if to cover as much of what was left of her identity as possible.

"Please raise your right hand to be sworn," asked the bailiff.

Mrs. Chow complied, swore to tell the truth, and sat down in the witness chair.

"Would you state your name and address for the record, please." Landau began the examination.

"My name is Thelma Chow. I live near Chinatown, but I prefer not to give my address, please."

"Why is that, Mrs. Chow?" Landau knew the reason and expected this response, but asked the question for effect.

"Please, I do not want him to know where I live." Mrs. Chow pointed to the defendant, and looked pleadingly at the judge.

"Mr. Boyd, is this witness's address necessary for the record?" The judge inquired.

"No, Your Honor." Boyd answered.

But Landau was now performing for more than the judge.

"The prosecution appreciates this witness's concern for her safety, and I will move on." Landau stated.

"Your Honor," Jackson Boyd stood up respectfully, "I object to Mr. Landau's commentary and to these planned theatrics for the press. This is a preliminary hearing, not a campaign speech." Boyd was bringing twenty years of experience to the defense of his client and was probably the highest paid black defense attorney in town. But this client could afford him. He had quite a backing.

"Yes. Mr. Landau, please proceed with the relevant questions." The judge agreed with Boyd.

"Ma'am, can you please tell us where you were on the night in question."

"I was driving home from the medicine shop in Chinatown. I had to pick up some remedy for my son."

"And did you see anything unusual happen?"

"I took a short cut through the alley, and I saw that man pushing another man against a wall, and holding a gun to his head. The other man was tied up and was trying to escape . . ."

"Let the record reflect that the witness has identified the defendant, Chan Ling. What did you see then?"

"I saw this man shoot the other man in the head when I drove into the alley. There was another man there, and my headlights flashed on them, and they saw me and ran. I went home and called 911."

"No further questions, Your Honor."

Landau concluded that this was all he needed to hold the case over for trial. The defendant has been identified by a percipient witness as the killer. One does not often have that type of direct evidence. And although Mitchell was always concerned for the safety of his witnesses in murder cases, especially when the defendants were as brutal as this one, he had DNA evidence that he was sure would tie Chan Ling to the alley murder. But the results took weeks to get back and Jackson Boyd was pushing the trial with the speed of a locomotive.

"Any cross, Mr. Boyd?" The judge asked.

"Yes, Your Honor. Mrs. Chow, what time was it that you saw these events you were just describing to the court?"

"It was just after 10:00 PM. The medicine shop closes at 10:00, and I remember that I just made it there before it closed."

"So, it would be fair to say that it was dark outside."

"Yes."

"Were there any street lights in the alley where these events took place?"

"I don't remember." Mrs. Chow answered honestly.

"Were there any lights shining into the alley where these events you described took place?"

"I really don't remember." Mrs. Chow answered.

"And as you testified, you just witnessed a man get killed, right?"

"Yes."

"Shot in the head."

"Yes."

"These are pretty scary events you are describing, Mrs. Chow."

"It was scary."

"You didn't get out of the car?"

"No."

"And you testified that after they saw you, they ran. True?"

"Yes."

"So, you only saw them for a fraction of a second, fair to say?" Boyd pressed.

"Yes, that's correct."

Jackson Boyd paused, evaluating whether he should pose the ultimate question, "Then how can you be so sure that this is the man?" It was a preliminary hearing, and he knew that what Landau presented was sufficient to hold his client over for trial. He also knew that, at trial, he would face physical evidence which would be difficult to overcome. Although the prosecution had yet to finish the

DNA analysis, it was his client's blood and hair fibers that were found on the back of the victim's head.

During the interview of his client, he asked Chan Ling directly whether the findings would link the murder to him. Some defense attorneys had a practice of never asking their clients about guilt. That way, they could put them on the stand to lie without breaching the canon of ethics. Boyd found this maneuvering hypocritical. The ethical rules could not have possibly been intended for the lawyer to have a need *not* to know. Jackson Boyd was not one of those lawyers. He not only asked his clients whether they did it, but grilled them on the details. He believed in knowing everything in order to properly conduct the defense. He simply would not put his clients on the stand. Period.

Chan Ling, with the calm of a priest taking a confession, explained to Boyd that the man he killed bashed the back of his head into his forehead trying to escape before Chan shot him. When Chan was arrested and booked, they photographed his forehead, which would close that evidentiary loop rather tightly.

There were ways of poking holes in this evidence, but, short of the hypocrisy, injustice, and stupidity that had combined to defeat the strength of such evidence in the O. J. Simpson trial, his client would be convicted despite Boyd's best efforts. Besides, this was L.A., and lightning does not and should not strike in the same place twice.

But perhaps he would get lucky and the DNA results would not materialize timely or, for some scientific reason beyond layperson's comprehension, turn out inconclusive. Then, Mrs. Chow would be the only percipient witness left connecting his client to the murder, and this was his opportunity to test the witness. To see how she would do at trial. The risk was that if she did well, and answered the ultimate question affirmatively, he would have a harder time negotiating a deal and the witness would likely stick to her testimony during the trial. But if he were successful in shaking her, even just a bit, he would be that much better off in getting a plea bargain.

At Georgetown Law School, Boyd's favorite professor teaching Evidence made a poignant example of a defense lawyer in a case where his client bit off the ear of a victim. He got the witness to admit that he did not see his client bite off the ear, but then asked that ultimate question, "Then how do you know he bit it off?" The witness answered, "Because I saw him spit it out."

"No further questions, Your Honor." Boyd decided.

"Any further witnesses for the prosecution, Mr. Landau?"

"None, Your Honor."

"I think we can dispense with argument, Counsel. This court finds that there is sufficient evidence to proceed to trial on the case of *People v. Chan Ling*. See my clerk, please, Counsel, for a trial date."

"Your Honor," Boyd requested the judge's attention. "I would like to bring up the matter of bail again."

"Bail has been denied, Mr. Boyd. I will not reopen arguments on this issue. It is a murder one case with special circumstances. We're in recess."

Before Chan Ling was taken away, Jackson Boyd whispered something to his client who nodded. Boyd approached Landau as he was packing his briefcase.

"Mitch, we need to talk. I think my guy has something to offer to make a deal worth your while."

"I doubt it." Landau responded confidently. "But I'll listen."

"We're going to need privacy for this one."

"All right. Let's go to my office."

"I think we're going to need more privacy than that."

Landau looked at Boyd inquisitively, but knew that no questions would be answered until they were completely alone. The men walked out of the courthouse, and proceeded to a courtyard nearby. They said nothing on the way. Sitting down on a park bench, Landau broke the silence:

"What's on your mind, Jackson? This is the first time in many cases we've had against each other that you find it necessary to catch a breath of fresh air with me."

"Mitch, you know me pretty well. You know that my clients are not exactly Boy Scouts, and I think you also know that my reputation as an attorney and my integrity are important to me. But my first duty is to my client. When Chan Ling first told me this, I didn't want to approach you, but I have no choice. I've got to do what's in the best interests of my client, no matter who he may be."

"I'm listening."

"For the information I may be able to give you, I want manslaughter and he's out in five years."

"You're asking a lot, my friend. Frankly, I can't imagine what you can give me that would justify such leniency."

"This is off the record, of course, and I don't want to hear this ever again. No one can know where this came from, Mitch."

"Do you really feel it's necessary to question my ability to keep confidences?" Mitch asked.

Boyd paused and looked around as if to make sure that no one was within ear shot. He then spoke slowly and quietly.

"You obviously know that my client has connections to the Chinese mafia. As you also know, the D.A.'s office has been trying to penetrate them for years. My guy can give you their 'bean counter.' Obviously, the 'bean counter' will give you the documents, and the documents will give you names."

"That's great, Jackson," Mitch rebuffed. "You want me to let one mafia hood go for a chance to maybe get papers that may contain some names. Give me a break."

"Look, this is where it gets a little touchy. Let's just say, hypothetically, that this 'bean counter' was seen at Bellinger's last fund-raiser."

Mitchell could have sworn his heart began palpitating, but he could not react quickly, or it could be political suicide.

"I am really surprised at you, Jackson. Do you honestly think that I would give up a murder conviction for personal gain? Your client is a cold blooded murderer, and I could not live with myself if I let him go after five years just for the possibility that it may help me get elected as the district attorney.

"And here is another part I don't get," Mitch continued, "and which causes me additional pause. Why would this guy give up someone who can lead us to his bosses, and why in the world would you encourage a deal that would tag the people paying your tab?"

"Well, that's the beauty of this, Mitch. It's not my people. It's a rival family. See, it's a win-win." Jackson answered.

"Just great. I should give your guy a walk and simultaneously participate in clearing your client's way to the head of the class. No way, Jackson."

"I thought you may react this way. I just want you to think about one thing, Mitch. Think of how important the Danny Berardo conviction has been to your campaign, and what going after the Chinese mafia can do. Besides, you can put away a lot more Chan Lings when you're the district attorney than when you are a prosecutor who lost the election to become a district attorney. How many more big trials do you think Bellinger will let you handle if he wins reelection? And if there is any truth to the fact that the 'bean counter' was grazing on hors d'oeuvres at Bellinger's fund-raiser, do you think you'll ever get another shot at the Chinese cartel?"

"It's still wrong. We may be able to discuss murder two. He does twelve." Mitch was softening.

"Sorry, that part is not negotiable. Manslaughter and five years. Otherwise, no deal."

"Then no deal." Mitch said.

Boyd had no choice. He thought twelve years was a gift, but his marching orders were crystal clear. The men who paid his bills needed Chan Ling back. He was their best enforcer and extremely loyal. Boyd headed for his car. Mitch headed for his office, walking distance from the courthouse.

The Invitation

On that Monday morning, Tess was in her office on the ground floor of a new building. Her window looked out onto a garden, which the building management meticulously maintained year-round. She was in a rut. Business was good. Her talents had served her well. But she was burnt out. She went through this periodically for a couple of weeks, but always bounced back. It has now been a month.

A month ago, she thought she was fine—that enough time had passed, that the pain had dissipated, and that she was ready for the new chapter in her life, without Tommy Simon. But every time she caught a glimpse of hope that the misery was finally over, she found herself slipping back.

After the breakup with Tommy, there were the expected stages of recovery. First, she was depressed and stayed in bed except when she absolutely had to work. Then, in an attempt to prove to herself that Tommy really was not all that great, she had decided to start dating again. Then came a few unsatisfactory blind dates, which just accentuated her loss. One in particular made her almost run back to Tommy, pride notwithstanding. That night, after the painfully boring dinner with Clarence Myers, the stock broker, she found herself driving over to Tommy's house in Playa Del Rey by the beach.

On the way there, she was actually hoping that she would find him with another woman. As painful as that would be to see, it would help her close that chapter of her life. She stopped just short of his driveway. The living room was visible through the large window. Tommy's car was in the driveway. He was home. Alone.

"What a freak," Tess mumbled to herself. "Now you're acting like a stalker. Get over it and move on." She drove away from their former love pad, and has not been back since.

Then came the bounce back into her job where she has remained since and, until a month ago, seemed content to accept as her existence. There was clearly nothing wrong with it. She did not need Tommy, or any man for that matter. She was a successful business woman and, if a man came into her life at some future point, that would be fine.

Tess shook herself out of her useless daydreaming and picked up the phone to call Jim Pane. She teasingly chastised him about sending over Parks to sell her an investment. Jim readily confessed:

"Tess, I know you said you were not interested when I described the investment to you, but I thought if Charlie Parks had an opportunity to describe it to you directly, you would see that this seems like a heck of a deal." He apologized if this caused any trouble. The last thing he wanted to do was make her life more complicated, but, now that she was making money, he thought it was important for her to think about investing.

Tess reassured Jim that he did nothing wrong, and thanked him for thinking about her as usual, and having her best interests in mind. But she was still building her business and the money she was making was going right back into it.

"Ms. Lowe," asked the female voice through the intercom.

"Yes." Tess answered.

"There is a man by the name of Charlie on the phone. He insists on speaking with you, and says you'll know what it's about."

"Thank you, Sylvia, I'll take it." Tess waited a few seconds before she picked up the phone.

"This is Tess Lowe."

"Tess, this is Charlie. Remember? Charlie Jamieson. We met at the showing last week. You must remember—I'm the one who made a fool out of myself and spilled wine on your beautiful new carpet. I must apologize for not giving your secretary my last name. I was afraid if I did, you wouldn't take my call. I'm calling to make restitution. Will you have dinner with me tonight?"

"I can't tonight, Mr. Jamieson, and there is no need for any restitution. The purchase you made quite suffices." Tess was visibly annoyed.

"What about Saturday night or any night next week. After that I'm leaving for Boston on business, and you won't get another shot at me for a month."

"Mr. Jamieson. I'm flattered, but I really must decline. I will let you know when my next showing is, and we can see each other then."

"Very well, Tess, but you will miss the time of your life!" fifty-year-old Jamieson exclaimed trying to save his fragile male ego.

"I'm sure that's true, and I *am* sorry. Goodbye."

Tess hung up the phone abruptly, surprising herself that she was actually upset that it was not Charlie Parks who called. What the hell was she thinking. This was ridiculous. She could not possibly be that desperate. Parks, of all people, a man who wreaked sales with every molecule of his being.

Her thoughts quickly turned to business, and she began methodically to attack the thick stack of papers on her desk. There was a knock on her door, and Sylvia entered the office holding a box of Winchell's donuts.

"Ms. Lowe. There is a young man here to see you without an appointment and he insisted that I bring you this box of donuts. I asked his name, but he sent me in here to ask you that since he brought donuts, would you change your mind about a cup of coffee."

"Thank you, Sylvia. You can let him in."

Charlie Parks walked into Tess's office to find her leaning back in her chair eating a glazed donut.

"You're persistent, Mr. Parks." She said.

"Glazed? I figured you for a jelly donut type." Charlie said.

"Too messy. Now, Mr. Parks, I understand that you came here to ask me to have coffee with you?"

"No. I am here to ask you to come over to my place for dinner."

27

"Then you got into my office under false pretenses. Is that how you sell your real estate investments too?"

"Now, look, Tess." Charlie tried to sound defensive. He had learned well that the secret to selling was not to sell, but to manipulate people into wanting to buy. There was no better way to accomplish that task than to keep pushing the product further and further away in conversation until, in that childish gesture of wanting what was no longer offered, the recalcitrant target became the willing victim.

"You don't know me from Adam," Charlie continued. "It's obvious that you've been taken by some sales person in the past and it made you cynical. But don't lump me into any categories. I don't like it. Besides, I frankly don't give a damn if you invest in The Oregon Project or not. In fact, given the choice between business and pleasure, and forgive me in advance for sounding piggish, but there is simply no question which one I would prefer with you. But I am secure enough to take no for an answer. Enjoy the donuts." Charlie turned and headed for the door.

"Do you cook?" Tess asked, stopping Charlie in his tracks.

"Do you like swordfish?" He answered with a question.

"Yes."

"I make a mean Cajun swordfish." Charlie said.

"I'm impressed."

"Don't be until you taste the food." Charlie walked back over to Tess's desk and placed his calling card in front of her. "My home address is on the back. How is 7:30 tonight?"

"That's fine. What can I bring?"

"Well, I must admit I'm not much of a wine connoisseur. Would you bring a bottle of wine with you?"

At that moment, Tess knew exactly which wine she would bring, which outfit she would select, and which perfume she would wear. The well deserved self-criticism she submitted herself to just minutes before was put aside. She was entitled to have fun. Besides, she could take care of herself. If it was all right to suffer through uneventful blind dates to get back on life's track after a breakup, it should be just fine to have dinner with the likes of Charlie Parks, who promised to be much more entertaining. After all, she was not marrying the man.

Ike

"Nothing. A big fat nothing." Newsome said removing his glasses and rubbing his eyes.

He and Ike Murdoch had been working late into the night in Bellinger's office doing computer runs on Mitchell Landau. Murdoch, an ex-cop turned private investigator, barely fit in the seat at the computer. He was probably a hundred pounds overweight and had pock marks on his face from teenage acne. He tried covering his face with all variations of facial hair, but a beard made him look like Santa Claus and a goatee made him look like Colonel Sanders.

Newsome had pulled Landau's personnel file from the D.A.'s office and, just as a precaution, was cross-checking the information Landau put on the employment application with the information on the computer. Bellinger liked to keep a tight watch on his assistants, especially those who looked like they might challenge him. He had snitches in the D.A.'s office who would report the information to Murdoch and to his predecessor, and they would enter it into the computer files. The information was rarely used, but it made Bellinger feel a lot more comfortable. He had similar files on the mayor and the chief of police, just in case, but those required a special password that Bellinger made up and only he and Newsome knew.

If Murdoch wanted to retrieve those files or work on them, he would have to have Newsome log on with Murdoch's back turned to him. Murdoch was always irritated by this lack of trust, but Newsome never questioned his boss, or any boss for that matter, and letting Murdoch have the password against Bellinger's instructions was not even a consideration. Murdoch also suspected that there were other files kept in that computer, but it was none of his business. He was being paid for snitching on other people, not on those who hired him and paid him. "Don't shit where you eat," was his life's motto, and he believed that it got him this far.

The information on Landau was checking out, and the frustration level was building. Top of his class in college. UCLA Law School. Law Review. The closest thing they found to a lie was that Landau reported on his job application that he had graduated in the top 20 percent of his class at UCLA, and it appeared to be top 24 percent. This would most likely be interpreted as healthy ambition, and it was certainly nothing to bring up during a campaign. Married for five years to a Kari Monroe-Landau, a woman he met in law school. One child. His credit report showed moderate spending habits with five credit cards between the two of them, two cars, one leased, one owned, and a house in Woodland Hills worth maybe $400,000. Excellent credit rating.

The only notation in his computer file from his years with the D.A.'s office was from a secretary who complained that Landau sexually harassed her. Newsome would normally jump at this information, but the same woman accused Bellinger of harassing her, and, getting nowhere with her complaints, quit and filed a workers' compensation claim for stress.

"You can't count on what's in the machine, Timmy. You've got to let me do some leg work. Let me follow him around, ask some questions, and see what I can come up with."

"You worry me, Ike. Remember, this isn't one of your intimidation jobs. Landau is smart, and this is a very sensitive issue. If he so much as smells what we're doing, he will use the press to nail Bellinger. Besides, with your stature you are hardly invisible."

"Don't you worry about me or my stature. I've been in this business many years. I know what I'm doing. So, do I have your okay or do you have to run and ask permission." Murdoch knew how to get to Newsome.

"I have all the permission I need. Do it, Ike, but please, be careful. By the way, what exactly are you planning on doing?"

"Whatever it takes to get the job done."

"I was afraid you were going to say that. Alright, listen, I need to work on the computer alone. Do me a favor and disappear for awhile."

"Fine. I guess I might as well get started on our boy Mitchell." Murdoch put on a baseball cap, grabbed a raddled briefcase, and left.

Alone in the office, Newsome punched in the password and pulled up a directory of names. He found one that said "George Stone" and pushed the "Enter" button on the keyboard. When the file came up on the screen, he pulled out a piece of paper from his shirt pocket and entered some information to the end of the file. He saved the changes and turned off the computer. Since all the necessary information was now in the computer memory, he took the piece of paper and burned it in the ashtray on the desk.

Brentwood Luxury Apartments

Tess arrived at the Brentwood Luxury Apartments at 7:15 PM. She drove around and pulled into the parking lot twenty minutes later and let a valet park her car. She was wearing a simple white dress with a zippered back and spaghetti straps running across her tan shoulders. She took the elevator to the ninth floor, found Unit 907 and knocked.

Charlie opened the door. Over gray pants and a silk white shirt with rolled up sleeves, he was wearing an apron.

"Tess, it's good to see you again. Come in." Charlie said welcoming her into his newly found home.

Charlie found this place on George's recommendation shortly after Jim Pane and three others made their "investments" in The Oregon Project. George lived up to his part of the bargain, and distributed Charlie's share to him—in cash. George was ready that day to pull out of the Stone-Takushi venture just as a good poker player knew when to quit. Besides, George had other ventures and other ideas, some ongoing and some still brewing in his head. The trick was never to stay in any one too long, or take too many people for too much money. Between Jim Pane and three others, they had brought in $325,000 in a matter of weeks. The overhead had been minimal, and George's personal exposure almost nonexistent.

George had fifteen years experience in this "business," but Charlie was new to any venture that succeeded. He salivated over his share of $100,000. This was more than all his other schemes put together brought in, and more than he made in a year selling Mercedes. He was not ready to let go. He had tasted success, and he wanted more. Charlie convinced George to give him two more months—one long enough for the first checks to hit the investor's mail boxes, and another one to sell more properties.

"You've got two months," George told him that day. "After that, Stone Enterprises and Takushi Investments are officially and forever out of business."

"I hope you like this wine." Tess handed Charlie a bottle of French White Bordeaux and followed him into the kitchen. There was nothing more attractive than a man who knew how to cook, she thought.

"By the way, where did you learn to cook?" She asked Charlie, who had taken out a Tupperware container from the refrigerator with what looked like homemade sauce.

"Believe it or not, a long time ago, I spent a year in New Orleans, working in the kitchen of a Cajun restaurant. I washed dishes, watched the chef, and ate the scraps. All in all, not a bad combination."

Charlie was telling the truth. What he omitted was that he did this under the name of Keith Williams after the feds got interested in his latest scheme. Charlie resumed his identity after the statute of limitations ran. Tess watched as Charlie placed two perfectly shaped pieces of swordfish into a glass pan filled with marinade from the Tupperware.

32

"I don't normally do this because it gives away my secrets," Charlie said as he filled a teaspoon with the marinade, and brought it to Tess's lips, "but I'd like to know what you think."

Tess took a sip. "Mm, that is delicious. What's in it?"

"If I told you that, I'd have to kill you." Charlie joked as he put the bottle of wine Tess brought into the refrigerator along with the fish, and pulled out a bottle of Cristal champagne.

"If you don't mind, Tess, I'd like to save the wine for dinner. But I do think we should celebrate."

"What are we celebrating?" Tess asked impressed with this man's impeccable taste.

Charlie handed Tess her glass and led her to the couch in the living room, furnished with white Italian leather. The coffee table was smoked glass. He'd always had the taste, but never had the money. Until now.

"Well, I know how you feel about the real estate business. But to tell you the truth, I just don't have anyone else to celebrate with. So, I'd like to share the good news with you. I know Jim Pane is a good friend of yours, and I hope that, if not for me, you will drink to his success."

"What's this all about?"

"Well, we're only eight properties away from selling the entire project. I'm meeting with the overseas representatives next week in Oregon to finalize the details."

"I'm sorry. I don't know much about your project. What does this mean?"

"The Japanese investors in The Oregon Project are very impressed with the speed these properties sold. They are talking about providing us with additional financing to expedite the completion of the project. That means that if the project is completed sooner, your friend, Jim, and all the investors, will see their returns that much sooner. Frankly, I wish I didn't have all my money tied up in the company itself or I would personally buy the eight remaining properties."

"You might as well tell me about this project, Charlie. You've been wanting to since the day you showed up at Palestine's. What the heck is it, anyway?" Tess asked.

Charlie pulled a rolled up drawing from the corner of the room, grabbed a folder from a shelf, and invited Tess to sit down at the table.

"What you see in front of you are photographs representing construction of a major real estate development in Oregon." Charlie pointed to photographs showing construction of individual homes. He then removed the photographs from the table and put them back in his briefcase. Instead, he spread out the artist's drawing of the completed project.

"This is what it will look like when it is completed. My company, Stone Enterprises, owns this land in Oregon. The concept, although simple, is quite brilliant and original: fifty single family homes made part of a self-contained community, called The Oregon Project. The homes are built in an arc," Charlie was pointing to the drawing.

"Here, in the center, is a private school, kindergarten through eighth grade, a supermarket, a movie theater, and a gas station. There is a park here with a place for children to play and a jogging track. This is the sports club, with a gym, tennis courts, Olympic size swimming pool, and two club houses—one for men and one for women. The entrance to the project is gated and guarded."

Charlie changed his tone of voice from business to personal. "Tess, you and I don't know each other, really, and you may not believe me when I say this, but this venture is very important to me. I have worked long and hard on making it a success. And that's exactly what it is—a success. Anyway, since I gather that you and Jim are good friends, I just wanted to let you know. Well, I think the fish is ready to cook." He refilled Tess's glass with more champagne, and said:

"Now, I refuse to be watched while I cook. You will just make me nervous, and I will undoubtedly do something to ruin dinner."

Charlie led Tess to the couch, pushed the button on the remote control of his new TV and turned it on for Tess.

"Is there anything else I can get for you at this time, ma'am?" Charlie said pretending to be a waiter draping a white kitchen towel over his left forearm.

"Oh, I think you've done quite enough already, sir. But I will let you know if I need anything else." Tess said sinking into the soft leather.

This was turning out exactly as she expected. Fun, entertaining, and Charlie was rather charming. The last two months of her three-year relationship with Tommy were accented by arguments and dissipating pleasure in each other's company. They were in love, that was not the issue, but their visions for the future were in conflict and some things simply cannot be compromised.

The TV program Tess was watching was interrupted with a commercial. In the ad, Grant Bellinger walks by the filled jail cells. Overlaid on the screen were percentages showing the great conviction record of his terms. Pointing to the inmates, Bellinger declared: "They say they have rights. Well, what about yours." The commercial ends with Bellinger walking out of the jail, holding his head high, and a voice reading the large print on the screen: "Bellinger, the only man tough enough to stand up for YOUR rights."

Half an hour later, Charlie announced that dinner was ready. They sat at the beautifully set candlelit dining room table surrounded by windows with a view of the city. Charlie did serve a mean swordfish, and Tess did pick the right wine. The Oregon Project was not discussed throughout dinner. They talked about Tess's business, and how she built it from the ground up. She explained her relationship with Jim. How he took a liking to her because she reminded him of himself, building a business by himself. They also shared a love of art, although not always with the same taste.

They talked about her house, and how the property values boom made it a great buy. They even talked briefly about Tommy Simon, and Charlie reassured Tess that it was Tommy's loss.

"Any man who would walk out on you doesn't deserve you." Charlie said as he got up to clear the table.

When he took the dishes into the kitchen, Tess stared at the spectacular city view and lost herself again. The evening was very nice, but, at the end of it, her thoughts went back to Tommy. She cursed herself for not being able to let go. She used to be so free, dating more than one man in a week, sometimes in a night. Some would call what she did promiscuous. She called it satisfying abandon. She was in control of who she was and with whom she would be. That is, until Tommy. For him, she not only gave up all others. That was easy. For him, she changed. And yet, he left.

"Would you like another glass of wine? I can open another bottle." Charlie asked, loading the dishwasher.

"I better not. I do have to drive home."

Charlie wiped his hands on the dish towel, and approached Tess. He put his hand on her face and caressed her cheek with the back of his fingers:

"You really don't have to drive home. I would like it if you stayed." There was an air of dominance and control in the way he asked.

Tess opened her mouth to respond. She expected the word "No" to come out, but, instead, she reached in and kissed him. And while the kiss came as a surprise to her, the old feeling of freedom was familiar and comforting. She knew what she was doing. There would be no hurt feelings, no arguments, no life-altering decisions.

Charlie put both arms around Tess, brought his hands to the middle of her back and gently pulled her in until their bodies meshed. They kissed long and hard, neither one wanting it to end.

When their first kiss was finally over, Charlie said,

"Tess, I want you. I wanted you since the first time I saw you. If you want to leave, I'll understand, but there is nothing I want more right now than to make love to you."

"That's more like it," Tess thought to herself. He took her hand and led her into the bedroom.

They stood two feet apart near the bed staring at each other. She wanted him to throw her on the bed and not let her breathe. Instead, Charlie stepped back and dimmed the lights.

"Take off your dress." He ordered unbuttoning his shirt.

"Don't you want to take it off?" Tess whispered.

"No. I want to watch you undress. Take it off slowly."

Tess, with excitement mounting inside her, reached across and slowly slid off one strap. As the strap fell off her shoulder, Charlie could see the outline of her dark nipple. Feeling his eyes on her breast, Tess licked her fingers and gently rubbed the exposed nipple.

Charlie took off his shirt and moved towards Tess, but only to be rebuffed:

"Not yet. You wanted to watch. So, watch."

Charlie obeyed and stepped back. Tess reached behind and unzipped her dress. It fell to the floor.

"You are more beautiful than I imagined." Charlie gasped, meaning every word.

Using both hands, Tess began touching herself. She gently caressed her breasts and then slowly and deliberately eased her way downward, finally resting her hand on her inner thigh, teasing herself and her voyeur. At last, when she put her hand inside her silk panties, Charlie stepped forward and wrapped himself around Tess's naked body. He kissed her mouth, her neck, her breasts, touching between her legs and feeling her excitement matching his. Entwined, they fell on the bed.

CHAPTER

The Gallery

At The Gallery Restaurant, Jim Pane and his niece, Milly Aaron, were going over the reservations list. It appeared that it would be a relatively quiet night. Jim pointed to a name on the 8:00 PM line that said "Mitchell Landau, party of two."

"This is probably our next district attorney." Jim said. "Give him the corner booth and a bottle of whatever it is they are drinking on the house."

"You know that means that, in the interests of equal time, we will have to send a bottle to his opponent," Milly joked.

"If he comes here for dinner and pays for the meal, he will get his free bottle." Jim really did have no sense of humor. "I cannot be around tonight, Milly. Esther and I are celebrating our thirtieth wedding anniversary, and I am expected home. If you need me for anything, just leave a message."

"Congratulations, Uncle Jim. That's great." Milly said. "Don't worry. I've got this handled. It's second nature to me now. You guys have a great evening and give Esther my best."

Milly's mother and Jim's sister died when Milly was only two years old, and she was brought up by her father, who was a well respected law professor at Loyola Law School. Milly was very close to her father and dependent on him emotionally. When Milly was

39

eighteen, her father died of prostate cancer. Samuel Aaron left a will, leaving the house to Milly and the rest of his estate, including a life insurance policy, in trust for her until she turned twenty-five. Two months ago, on Milly's twenty-fifth birthday, Milly came into possession of the remainder of the trust, and almost immediately parted with most of it on her uncle's recommendation.

"You are a godsend." Jim responded. "I don't know if I could manage this place without you. Alright, then. I will see you tomorrow." Jim palmed a bottle of wine he had selected from the cellar for the anniversary celebration and headed out of the restaurant.

At 8:00 PM, Mitchell Landau walked into The Gallery with his wife, Kari. They walked up to the maître d' and announced their arrival. Kari, with her stunning olive skin and black eyes, was a perfect compliment to Mitch's pale skin accented by a few remaining freckles. Kari inherited her father's strength of character and her mother's Latin temper. She had perfect posture and exuded confidence and personality.

Milly greeted them personally and escorted them to the corner booth.

"Mr. and Mrs. Landau, my name is Milly Aaron. I manage The Gallery. Jim Pane, the owner, is very pleased that you are dining here tonight, and is sorry that he could not be here personally to welcome you, but he and his wife are celebrating their wedding anniversary. Your waiter will be with you momentarily, and whatever you are drinking is on the house."

"That's very generous, Ms. Aaron, and thank you, and thank Mr. Pane for us, please." Mitchell replied.

"That's awfully nice," Kari quipped sarcastically when they were alone. "You were right, Mitch. There are fringe benefits to an otherwise miserable existence as the wife of a district attorney."

"Kari, please." Mitch answered. "I know things are crazy, but we talked about this before I decided to run. Nothing is happening that isn't par for the course in these things. I am still behind in the polls and if we don't close the gap, this whole thing will be for naught.

Worse, Bellinger will undoubtedly make my life miserable if he wins. So, what I could really use right now is you on my side."

"I am on your side, Mitch. And please don't patronize me. I may not be practicing law any more, but I am not stupid. You say you want me on your side, but you shut me out from everything that is your side. You relegate me to your meal and sleeping partner but expect my support." Kari stopped talking when the waiter brought the wine to the table.

He twirled the bottle to show off the label and, with Mitch's permission, poured the wine for him to taste.

"My wife is the connoisseur." Mitch said to the waiter, who promptly apologized and poured a taste in Kari's glass. Kari smiled at her husband, recognizing the small, but clearly conciliatory move, chewed the wine and looked at Mitch playfully with her mouth full. He looked back at his gorgeous spouse, somewhat nervous as to whether she would carry out this playful threat. It was her natural ability to crosscut the seriousness of the moment with a joyful touch that he loved so much about her.

"This will be fine. Thank you." Kari finally said to the waiter who poured the wine into both glasses and left.

Mitch held his wife's hand under the table. "Look, Kari, I know I have been less than a good partner lately."

"That's putting it mildly." Kari interrupted.

"The election is clearly putting a big strain on our marriage. But we will come through this. Just like we came through everything else in our relationship."

"Mitch. This isn't about our relationship. That implies that I have something to do with this. This one is entirely on your shoulders. This one is all about you." Kari said quietly so as not to telegraph their fight to the next table.

"What does that mean?"

"It means that I will not stay married to someone who is slowly but surely transforming into one of those men who does not talk to his wife, plays golf with his buddies on his days off, exchanging highly exaggerated stories of their latest sexcapades, and acts superior to the opposite sex."

"I'm not like that, Kari. How can you even say that."

"Mitch. You are not like that now, but I see the signs. You leave for work without so much as sharing a cup of coffee with me or telling me what's in store for you during the day. You call me once during the day to let me know when you will be home, and when you get home, you barely say a word to me. All in all, you make me feel like some Stepford wife. Mind you, I did better than you in law school, and . . ."

"Honey, you don't need to do that. I know how smart you are, and you are a heck of a lawyer. I'm sorry. I didn't know you felt that way." Mitch said.

"And whose fault is that?" Kari asked.

"Alright. I'm sorry, Kari. I know we used to be a team."

"We can be again, Mitch. I feel awful saying this, but there is a part of me that would not be so devastated if you lost. Maybe we can finally do what we've talked about for years."

"Kari, I am not ready to do defense work. You know that this is my dream. I've been wanting this for so long, I can taste it." Mitch lifted his glass of wine and toasted his wife.

"To the most incredible, the most beautiful, the smartest wife in the world."

"You're an asshole," Kari said jokingly, resigning herself to the fact that this argument would, like many others in their recent history, be tabled until this election was over.

When Milly returned to the front of the restaurant after seating the Landau party, she noticed a large man walk in through the front door and head for the bar. He chose a seat in the back facing the dining room and ordered a drink. He seemed out of character for The

Gallery, but he was a paying customer. Milly paid no more attention to him and kept to her management responsibilities for the night.

At the back of the bar, Ike Murdoch sipped his scotch rocks. He followed Mitch from the office to the Landau home and then to the restaurant. He was not sure what he was looking for, but that was the great thing about this job. Nothing one minute and something the next. Besides, getting forty dollars an hour for drinking booze was a no lose proposition.

Ike Murdoch watched Mitch and Kari Landau drink the bottle of wine and then order snifters of cognac for an after dinner drink. Suddenly, he had an idea.

When they were done with dinner, Mitch and Kari walked outside the restaurant, hand in hand, into the fresh L.A. evening air. So much of their lives were spent inside that the few and far between moments outside, even if it was waiting for the car, were somehow invigorating and calming at the same time. Mitchell handed the ticket and a five-dollar bill to the valet, and he and Kari got inside their car and drove away. But the Landau's Audi was barely a mile away from The Gallery when their rear view mirror was flooded with red lights.

"What the hell is going on?" Mitch cursed. "Maybe they just want my autograph."

"This is no time to joke, Mitch. Why would they be pulling us over?"

The Audi stopped, and as the cop came up to the driver's side, the tinted window came down, revealing a concerned but cooperative face of Kari Landau, the driver.

"May I see your driver's license and registration, please ma'am?" said the cop shining his flashlight inside the vehicle.

Mitch opened the glove compartment, and pulled out the registration as Kari took out her driver's license from her wallet.

"Officer, I am Assistant District Attorney Mitchell Landau, and not that I am seeking any special treatment, but I must say I am confused as to why we are being stopped."

43

The cop directed his flashlight at Landau and immediately turned it off.

"Gee, I'm sorry, Mr. Landau, but we got a phone call that an Audi with your license plate had left The Gallery restaurant and was weaving on the road, like there was a drunk driver. The caller said it looked like you were going to hit someone or run into something. We were in the area, so we got the call."

"Well, officer, my wife and I did have some wine with dinner, but I would hardly say that we are drunk, and we certainly were not weaving. The caller must have been drunk." Mitch was quickly putting the pieces together. "If you want to administer the breathalyzer test to my wife, I assure you she would be well within the legal limit." Kari, tonight's designated driver, was rather reserved in her alcohol consumption at the restaurant, tasting more than drinking.

"That won't be necessary, sir." The cop returned the license and registration to Kari. "I am sorry sir, ma'am, I was just doing my job."

"We understand, officer." Kari replied. "May we go now?"

"Certainly." The cop said as he returned to his vehicle.

Pulling away from the curb, Kari looked over at her husband who was grinding his teeth.

"Would you vote for a district attorney who was arrested for drunk driving?" Mitch asked rhetorically. "They want to take the gloves off? Fine, we'll just see who ends up with a black eye."

"Be careful, Mitch. This is how things get out of control. I know you want to win this election, but at what cost."

"Kari, what do you want me to do? Take this shit? That's just not me, and you know that. Don't ask me to be less than who I am."

"I'm not, Mitch. I am asking you to be exactly who you are. Don't go down to his level. You are better than that. Bellinger is a fucking monster. You and I both know that. Or have you forgotten that I had to quit the D.A.'s office because you and I were dating. When he is threatened, he fires, and you are now his favorite target."

Mitch knew that Kari was right. She was always right. That was the most irritating thing. Worse, when he would admit that she was right, instead of dropping the subject, she would simply say, "I know I'm right. That's not the issue." But as frustrating a characteristic as that may be in your partner in life, she was his biggest fan, his staunchest supporter, and . . . she was right.

"I need to run something by you." Mitch said as they drove home. "Jackson Boyd approached me after court today. He offered me a plea in exchange for information which could, for all intents and purposes, end Bellinger's career."

"Why haven't you told me this yet, Mitch."

"I know, Kari. I should have. And you've made your point."

"What's the information?" Kari asked switching gears, as she did so many times, from unsatisfied spouse to the "all hands on deck" partner.

Mitch told Kari about the conversation he had with Jackson. About the information he could get by arresting the "bean counter," including that Bellinger's coffers were filled with illegal campaign contributions.

"But, in the end, I turned it down." Mitch concluded. "I'm thinking now I may have been too quick."

They talked this through all the way home, considering all the scenarios, running all the possible outcomes to ground. This was the old Mitch and Kari. Two assistant district attorneys, working cases together, brainstorming into the night, each smarter than the other, each with a passion for law, and, with time, for each other. When they got home, they spent the night as husband and wife, partners in life, well matched souls traveling the same path, and not as the candidate for district attorney and his weary spouse.

The Morning After

When Tess awoke the next morning, she was alone in Charlie's apartment. She got dressed and sat on the edge of the bed. The alarm clock said that it was 8:15 AM. She had no idea where Charlie had gone nor when he would be back. She enjoyed the fact that this did not phase her. Tommy may have been gone, but she was back. Tess decided to write Charlie a note.

"Thank you so much for the wonderful time, in and out of bed." She reached into her purse, took out a tiny bottle of perfume, put a drop on her finger, and rubbed it on the note, a trick she learned from some trashy novel she read on a beach one summer, the name of which she could not now recall. Considering her history, it was amazing to her that she had gone without sex for a year. She had been with no one since Tommy. Prior to him, she could not recall going a month without a sexual encounter, if that long.

In college, she actually kept score of the number of men she had been with, and notched a trophy she got in some school athletic competition after each new conquest. This was simply something she needed in her life again, she reasoned, as she left Charlie's apartment.

Charlie returned home from his morning jog to find that Tess had already gone. He was disappointed. Running always invigorated him and he wanted to make love to her again. He found the note on his pillow, smelled the perfume, and smiled.

Tess arrived home twenty minutes later. She put the coffee on to brew and got in the shower. She leaned against the shower wall and let the hot water run on her face. She could still smell Charlie on her body and was sorry to see the scent disappear with the soap. The night was wonderful. Charlie was passionate one minute, gentle the next. When he was on top, he stretched her arms over her head and pushed them into the bed. He leaned over her ear and told her not to move. He covered her body with his and rocked her insides and her world. When she was on top, he relegated everything to her, and she took to her task with glutinous longing.

When Tess got to the office an hour later, a message from Charlie was already on her desk. She returned the call.

"I wanted to apologize for letting you wake up alone this morning." Charlie said. "It's been a habit of mine to run every morning. It allows me to work out the animal in me."

"Judging by last night, I think you have to increase your mileage." Tess said.

"I'd like to see you again." Charlie said. "Would this evening be too soon?"

"I'd love to," Tess responded without hesitation, "but under one condition. You come to my place and let me cook for you."

"I can't think of a better offer."

"Great. 7:00 o'clock O.K.?"

"Yes. I need your address and directions."

Tess finished giving the directions to Charlie, hung up the phone, and began to plan the evening in her mind.

Charlie was right on time. He pulled into the driveway of Tess's house at exactly 7:00. He took the white long stem roses from the seat next to him and headed for the door. Taped to the front door was a folded note with his name on it. At first, he thought he was being stood up, but then he read the note:

"The door is unlocked. Go into the dining room where you will find further instructions on the table. Tess."

Charlie opened the door and walked into the dining room. On the table he found an ice bucket with a bottle of Dom Perignon and two empty champagne glasses. He put the roses down and picked up his next set of instructions which were leaning against the ice bucket.

"Open the champagne, fill the glasses and head down the hall into the second room on your right."

47

The second room on the right was the bedroom. On the bed, Charlie found another note with his name on it. He put the champagne glasses on the night table, and read:

"Take off your clothes and come in through the door on the left. Don't forget the champagne."

Charlie stripped naked. The lights in the room to the left were turned off and the room was lit by a single candle. He could see the large sunken tub filled with bubbles. He walked in and placed the champagne glasses on the ledge of the tub, feeling his way in the semi-darkness. He felt Tess's hands wrap around him from behind and could feel her naked breasts touch his back. He turned around and kissed her passionately. When their lips finally separated, Charlie picked Tess up, lowered her into the soapy water, and kneeled at the edge of the tub.

"You are incredible." Charlie said kissing the back of Tess's neck. "If your appetizer is this good, I can't wait to taste the dinner."

"Well," Tess said softly with a coy smile. "I hate to be the bearer of bad news, but I can't cook. I thought we would just order pizza later."

"I can't believe you lied to me." Charlie said teasingly, and poured a bit of cold champagne onto her shoulder as punishment. Tess shuddered from the contrast between the hot water and the cold champagne.

"O.K., O.K. I repent. No more lies. We'll put any toppings you want on the pizza."

"Good. No anchovies," Charlie said climbing into the bathtub. "But food is not exactly what I have on my mind at the moment."

They made love in the soapy water. Much quicker than the night before, dispensing with foreplay and the visual candy of seeing each other's bodies for the first time. The erotic play they enjoyed last night was exchanged readily and willingly by both for the sheer pleasure of sex, of body parts connecting and conjoining just long enough to bring their rightful owners to those few seconds that so frequently define the relations between the sexes. When they released each other, each retreated into the opposite side of the large bathtub, like boxers after finishing a round.

Tess lifted a glass of champagne left at the side of the tub, took a sip and asked with a satisfied smile, "So, how was your day?"

"Pretty fucking excellent." Charlie answered. "In fact, I'm afraid I have to be at work really early in the morning, and couldn't stay the night. I'm sorry."

"Well, that's rather presumptuous of you, thinking I was going to ask you to stay." Tess said still feeling sexy and flirtatious. "But, on the slim chance that I was going to invite you, why can't you stay?"

"I have to meet with one of the investors in The Oregon Project early in the morning. He is getting a second mortgage on one of his properties to finance part of his investment, and we need to go over some paperwork."

"Getting a second mortgage? That seems like a rather extreme measure for an investment?"

"Well, this guy feels that with the interest rates being as low as they are right now, and with the guaranteed monthly return on his Oregon investment, he can make a substantial profit and use the monthly checks to make payments on the second mortgage. He's got plenty of cash, but he thinks he'd rather use the bank's money to make this profit. In fact, this guy is buying out the last four properties. After that, we're done."

"So, I guess it would be too late for me to invest." Tess said. "To tell you the truth, between you and Jim, you guys have peaked my interest. But all my money is tied up in my business. I didn't think of getting a second on my house. I must have $200,000 to $250,000 equity. Sounds like it would have been a smart investment." Tess said, getting out of the tub and wrapping a towel around herself. Charlie watched as his appetite for Tess rose again. He had to shake himself back to his real purpose for his wonderful encounters.

"Tess, look, this guy already has four other properties and frankly, I would much rather see you make this money than him. If you think you may want to do this, tell me, and I'll try to put the brakes on this purchase for awhile. I'll make something up."

"How much time would I have to get the loan through?" Tess asked, handing a towel to Charlie as he got out of the tub.

"If you tell me you're going to do this, I can buy you a couple of weeks perhaps. I know that's not much time, but I have to make the meeting with Takushi in Oregon. It's scheduled for September 5, and by that time I have to have the remaining properties sold."

They called for pizza, settling on pepperoni and mushrooms, and ate it in bed. Tess made a pot of coffee before Charlie left.

"How do you take it?" She asked.

"Black with sugar."

"You know one thing I don't get about this Oregon Project you're working on," Tess said, "Why not buy real estate here in Los Angeles?"

"That's because you're not buying a piece of real estate by yourself," said Charlie recognizing the standard question. "It's actually a pretty ingenuous business plan. Wish I could take credit for coming up with it, but I was just hired to help implement it." That part was certainly true, Charlie thought.

"See, the thing is that you are not buying a piece of real estate by yourself. There is a Japanese company, Takushi Inc. The Asian markets have been hit hard. They want to invest in U.S. real estate, but they want Americans to front the money and act as partners. They have entered into an agreement with us. Jim has a copy of it." Charlie drank Tess's coffee with gusto.

"The beauty of it is that one of Takushi Inc.'s subsidiaries is Takushi Bank. The deal we made with them is this: As we sell each individual property, they agree to provide the financing to complete its construction. When we sell all fifty properties, they will finance the rest of the construction of The Oregon Project.

"And when it's completed, Takushi's other newly formed subsidiary, Takushi Investments Ltd., will buy The Oregon Project from Stone Enterprises at an agreed-upon price. At that point, the investors have a choice—you can either keep your individual properties, and do with them as you wish, or sell your property and receive twice the amount of your investment in return."

"But if Takushi has its own bank, why do they need investors?" Tess asked.

"Well, Takushi is not convinced that there is interest in the project. They do not want to jump in with both feet until they are assured of the success of the venture. So, their safeguard is that, unless all fifty properties are sold, they don't have to shell out the rest of the money for completing the project. If, on the other hand, all fifty properties are sold, they will feel quite comfortable in taking over and running the project."

"I still don't understand why they would guarantee to double the investors' money when they are financing the properties. Doesn't make sense." Tess said.

"We insisted on it. If they expected us to go out and find investors and make representations to the investors, we wanted guarantees. They agreed." Charlie finished.

"Listen, Tess, I'm sorry, but I have go to. I will call you later." Charlie kissed Tess on the lips, and said, "Here, let me leave this file with you. It's got all the details on The Oregon Project, if you want to look at it."

The next morning, Tess sat alone in her living room. She was not quite ready to go to work. She called Sylvia and told her she would be in the office in a couple of hours. She opened the folder Charlie left, and began to read the contents.

Construction cost for each home in The Oregon Project was estimated at $250,000, said the business plan. Exhibit A contained the recent figures on building costs in Oregon, and concluded that the state was one of the least expensive places to build homes from the ground up.

The minimum investment was $25,000 per home. Stone Enterprises carried the remainder of the construction loan directly with Takushi Bank, and the investors were indemnified from any liability or responsibility for the loan. Attached as exhibit B was a copy of the global agreement with Takushi, including subexhibits containing the indemnities mentioned.

The investors were expected to take the loan over only when the project was completed and, even then, it was the investors' choice whether to keep the property. Attached as exhibit C was a sample agreement with each investor, with only the name, the address of the particular lot, and the amount of the investment left blank.

Next, was the joint commitment from Stone Enterprises and Takushi Investments Ltd. to pay each investor a monthly return of 3 percent on the investment. As an example, the business plan went on to explain, if one invested $25,000, he or she would receive a monthly check for $750.00 for a year, guaranteeing a minimum return after one year of 36 percent. If the deal went through as expected, Takushi bought the project, and the investor wanted to sell his or her ownership interest, Takushi would pay an extra 64 percent return to guarantee doubling of the investment amount. If, instead, the investor chose to keep the property, he or she got to keep the money already received.

Finally, the business plan concluded, to encourage investors to buy as many properties as possible, four properties would increase the return to 5 percent monthly. So, the example demonstrated, if one invested $100,000, he or she would receive a monthly check for $5,000. If the investor then wanted to sell the properties to Takushi when the project was sold, they would pay the investor the extra $40,000.

Tess reviewed the copy of the Takushi agreement, which must have been at least fifteen pages in length, and flipped through the pages. On the last page were several signatures followed by corporate seals. She next reviewed the deed to the Oregon land. It had the county recorder's stamp on it.

Steven

In the back corner of the Beverly Hills branch of the First National Bank, the sign on the desk read "Steven Lowe, Vice President." A balding man in his mid-forties, wearing a blue suit with a yellow tie, walked out of a back office and headed towards the desk.

"Steven, vice president. When did this happen?" Tess said as she hugged her brother.

"Well, Sis, that's what you get for not checking up on your big brother more often." Steven complained superficially, since he was thrilled to see his baby sister.

"If I am not mistaken, the phone works both ways." Tess replied.

"I never could win an argument with you." Steven laughed. "To what do I owe this unexpected pleasure?"

"Actually, this is more business than pleasure. But now that you are VP, do I need to make an appointment?"

"No, Tess, seriously, for you I have all the time in the world. What's on your mind?" Steven asked.

"Well, without getting into too much detail, I was wondering how long it would take to get a second mortgage on my home."

"Usually, four to six weeks, if everything checks out okay. How much did you want to borrow?" Steven asked.

"$100,000."

"That's a lot of money, Tess. Is everything okay?" Steven was concerned.

"Everything is great. In fact, it hasn't been this good in a long time. I just found a great investment. Jim has invested in it, and it seems to be doing quite well, so I've decided to take some of the equity in my home and let it work for me." Tess explained.

"Always the business woman, Tess. Look, I probably could push it through a little quicker. When do you need the money?"

"I was hoping to be able to get it within two weeks."

"That's pushing it, but let me see what I can do." Steven reached into the drawer of his desk and pulled out a packet containing a loan application.

"Get these papers filled out and return to me as soon as possible. I'll go ahead and set the wheels in motion. I'll need to get an appraisal done on your house and a few other things. Do you think you can get the paperwork back to me by the day after tomorrow?"

"Of course. I really appreciate this." As Tess reached over to kiss her brother goodbye, she noticed the photograph of his wife and son on his desk. "Steven, I'm sorry. I didn't even ask about the family. God, look how Josh has grown. He looks like his handsome father. How is Terri?"

"Terri is busy as usual. It seems as though I barely see her since she made partner, but she's happy and that's what matters. Now, Josh, you'd be amazed, Tess. At fourteen, he is better with computers than I am. He has basically computerized our house. You really should stop by and see what he's done. Besides, I know Terri would love to see you."

"That's a great idea. How about if I bring the papers over to your house tomorrow night and you guys can feed me a home cooked meal?" Tess asked.

"Wonderful."

"Well, see you tomorrow night. And, Steven, thanks for this." Tess said pointing to the loan package.

Steven watched his sister leave and realized how much he had missed her. Ever since they moved to L.A., they had barely kept in contact with each other. They telephoned on birthdays and holidays, and occasionally got together for dinner. With the rest of the family back in Washington, Steven often missed the closeness in which the Lowes grew up. Ten kids in all, now spread all over the country.

He and Terri wanted more children, but after Josh, there were two miscarriages and he could not bear to watch Terri go through another one. The subject had been closed for several years.

When they offered him this branch, it was an offer he could not refuse. Tess, all of twenty at that time, followed him. After all, with art as your calling, it was either New York or Los Angeles. At first, she called him often for advice, a feeling that Steven treasured, but then, as a boat lifting its anchor for no reason other than it is simply time to go, Tess blossomed and never looked back. Now, she needed his help again, albeit in a perfunctory kind of way, and Steven was glad.

Steven picked up the phone and made arrangements for an appraiser to be at Tess's house at eight o'clock Friday morning.

CHAPTER 4

Century Escrow

At 9:00 AM on Tuesday morning, ten days after his rather enjoyable treasure hunt with Tess, Charlie pulled into the parking lot of Century Escrow on Wilshire Boulevard. The business of The Oregon Project was to be conducted there. Charlie remembered how happy he was making his first sale on this rather intriguing setup.

Jim Pane was the right target. He was a busy businessman at retirement age. Because he was busy, he likely did not handle his own books, and thus they would have another layer through which to traverse the scheme.

"This seems like an impediment," Charlie had asked George. "Isn't it easier to deal with one person."

"That's where you're wrong, Charlie." George had explained. "The more layers, the better. People love to cover their asses, and having someone else to point the finger at is always a plus. Besides, if he gets this thing approved by his CPA firm, when he learns of the scheme, he will go after them first, removing us that much further from the fray. They have insurance and will likely settle for enough to get this guy off our backs."

Because Jim was retirement age, he had cash on hand. Older people always liked to keep cash around and, ironically, did not trust banks, but would readily succumb to a sales pitch if it promised safety and security during their golden years.

Then came Milly Aaron. They were not expecting her, and, at her age and circumstance, she was not sought out. But Jim Pane brought her in. He called Charlie shortly after their meeting, and asked if they could accommodate another investor. Charlie said he would have to check, but Jim, anxious to share his find with those around him, promised that he would make it easy on Charlie. He would personally deliver the paperwork to Milly, and do whatever would make it easier to get her in.

There were three others who fit Jim Pane's description, and they also had signed on. Today, Tess Lowe would become the proud owner of vacant land in Oregon.

"You need a new suit," said George snidely as Charlie walked into the back office. "Takushi would not approve."

"Takushi, my ass, George. I am growing impatient with our arrangement. I am doing all the work, and you are sitting back collecting most of the dough."

"Don't lose your cool, Charlie." George said leaning back in his chair. "Remember who's paying all the bills. I even paid for that suit you're wearing. So you better turn on that charm or you'll be back at Johnson Mercedes where I found you."

The men heard the front door open, and Charlie went to check. It was Linda Sanders, the receptionist. Charlie and Linda exchanged "good mornings," and Charlie returned to the back office.

"It's Linda," Charlie reported.

"Oh yeah," said George taking yet another opportunity to drive home the point, "and I'm paying for her too."

Ten minutes later, Linda announced that Tess Lowe was in the lobby. Charlie asked Linda to show Tess into his office. George watched intently through the one-way mirror. The mirror installation was probably the most expensive item of overhead on the "Oregon Project," but as much as George liked to keep the overhead low, he found this a worthy investment. He refused to let Charlie—or anyone else for that matter—transact the money part of the business without him. Although the plan was not foolproof, it made him feel safer that Charlie was not outsmarting him and taking money from these investors without reporting it.

In the room on the other side of the mirror, Tess was handing over a cashier's check for $100,000 to Stone Enterprises, and Charlie was finalizing the escrow documents for her. Tess expected Charlie to be a little more personal during this transaction. After all, she was starting to lose count of the number of times they had made love. And while their arrangement was governed by unspoken understanding of its own limitations, she was still entitled to an acknowledgment of their short but intense history. Charlie was all business.

"Just sign here, Tess, and we are all set." Charlie said handing her a pen. Tess complied.

"Congratulations. You've got the last four properties of The Oregon Project. It is now officially sold out." Charlie reached out his hand to Tess meaning to shake hers. Tess took his hand, pushed it gently onto the desk, covering it with hers.

"Charlie, is something wrong or are you just working too hard?"

"Nothing is wrong, Tess. You're right. I am a little tired."

"Listen, I have a great idea." Tess said with forecasting excitement. "That trip to Oregon on September 5, it falls on a Thursday. Let's make a weekend out of it. You can meet with Takushi on Thursday, finalize the details, and we can spend the weekend celebrating."

Tess's enthusiasm was quickly doused when Charlie took his hand quickly from under hers.

"I don't think that's a good idea. This is an extremely important business trip. I will probably spend the entire weekend with the Takushi people. We have a lot of business to conduct. I will see you when I get back. We'll do something. I promise."

This dismissal stung Tess. Charlie was being borderline rude, and the ire responsive to this disrespectful conduct was rising in Tess.

But was she really upset at Charlie or was she superimposing his actions on Tommy. Who the hell knew? The most important thing was not to care. Besides, Tess told herself, this was her old stomping ground. Men coming in and out of her life. She had fun, and if it went no further, it served its purpose.

She reached across the desk and kissed Charlie on the lips. He returned the kiss.

"Call me." Tess said as she was walking out the door.

"I will." Charlie answered.

When she was gone, Charlie stacked the papers with the cashier's check on top. He looked into the mirror, knowing that George was watching him, and raised his brows in a celebratory gesture. It was so easy now. Almost routine. No guilt. No excuses. To the contrary, he had a repertoire of reasons why there was nothing wrong with what he did. After all, it was only money. He was no worse than the government taking taxes from hard working families and spending it on bureaucratic bullshit. And he took money from those who could afford it and would barely miss it. Robin Hood, in a way.

"Are you out of your fucking mind?" George greeted his partner when Charlie walked into the back office.

"What? I didn't reveal anything dangerous. I gave her the story about the meeting with Takushi to put a time deadline on her investment. Remember, you only gave me two months." Charlie sat down and lit a cigarette.

George grabbed the cigarette out of Charlie's mouth, and put it out on the metal edge of the desk.

"I am not talking about that. I figured when you told me you were making progress with her, that you were charming her, that maybe you slept with her once. You've got a goddamn relationship going with this woman." George was furious.

"I do not. I did only what I had to do to get her money. Isn't that what you wanted?"

"Oh, it's what I wanted all right. But not at the risk of having anyone get this close to you. I thought you were smart, Charlie. Now I have my doubts. What do you think the princess is going to do when her investment checks stop coming and you disappear? I knew I should have trusted my instincts and stopped this thing after the first round."

"Don't worry about it, George. My ass is on the line too. I won't do anything to jeopardize our business relationship." Charlie picked up the cigarette from the desk, and relit it. He needed to look cool and convincing.

"Our business relationship? You've got a lot to learn, my boy. You can't fuck and steal from the same person." George began to pace. "People you steal from just lose money, and they eventually give up on it. When the cops tell them it's a civil case, and they can't find the person to sue, they decide to write it off on their taxes and forget it. People you sleep with and steal from never forget. It's not the money they'll be after, it's revenge. Pack it up right now. Your share of the money will be in your account in two days as agreed. Keep your apartment for two more weeks, it's prudent. But officially, Stone Enterprises and Takushi are out of business as of today, you understand?"

Charlie understood. "What do I tell Tess?" He was looking for suggestions.

"Tell her that because the construction on The Oregon Project was being expedited, you have to spend a lot of time there supervising the business, and that after a couple of months, you may have to actually move there. That way, the move won't seem so sudden, and it will give us some time to cover our tracks. And do it on the phone, Romeo. Don't see her again."

"Okay." Charlie understood his instructions.

George put the cashier's check in the inside pocket of his jacket and headed out the door.

"What about my money?" Charlie asked following George into the parking lot.

61

"I have never welshed on a business deal." George retorted. "I told you, it will be in your account, as agreed."

"Charlie." The men heard a woman's voice. It was Tess, and she was walking towards them.

"Oh, shit." George cursed. "I thought she'd be long gone."

"Let me handle this," Charlie volunteered.

"Tess," Charlie said. "Is everything O.K.?"

"I can't seem to get my car started and my car phone won't turn on. I was just on my way in to see if I can use your phone."

"Of course you can. By the way, Tess, this is Walter Manning, another one of the investors in The Oregon Project. Walter, this is Tess Lowe. She just purchased the remaining four properties in the project."

"It's nice to meet you, Mr. Manning." Tess said.

"Same here," George answered. "Well, I better get going. I have a meeting to make." He got into his Mercedes and rolled down the window. "Ms. Lowe, I hope to see you again when we are both rich from this investment. Charlie, I thank you again for all your help."

"You are quite welcome, Walter. Anything I can do, you know where to find me."

"That I do," said George.

When they were alone, Charlie said, "Tess, I'm sorry if I was cold to you, but everything is coming to a head, and I just can't allow anything to go wrong. You understand, don't you?"

"Of course, I do. Look, just do what you need to do to prepare for this meeting, and then we'll celebrate when you come back from Oregon."

"Thank you." Charlie said. "Come on, let's see what's wrong with your car."

The Little Pig

That night, when Hsiao Tzu, the man formerly known as one grazing on hors d'oeuvres at Bellinger's fund-raiser, opened his laundry, appropriately called "The Little Pig Chinese Laundry and Dry Cleaning," he was confronted by two LAPD officers who served him with a search warrant and told him to come downtown for questioning. He put up the appropriate verbal resistance, questioning the officers on why he was being arrested.

"You are not being arrested, Mr. Tzu," the detective advised.

"It's Mr. Hsiao, thank you, and so why do I need to come with you?"

"Because if you don't, you will be arrested. How is that?" The smart-ass cop explained.

At the station, Hsiao was put into Interrogation Room 5 while crates filled with documents seized from his business were emptied in Interrogation Room 6 and divided into piles on the metal desk.

It was unusual for a prosecutor to question a suspect before he was charged, and by that time, they usually had lawyers who invariably told them not to speak to anyone. But this was different. Mitch insisted on doing this one himself. He had his reasons. If any eyebrows were raised, he would explain that this was all part of the Chan Ling plea bargain and he was simply verifying the facts as given to him by Chan Ling's lawyer. And while Hsiao Tzu was sweating it out, Chan Ling was on his way to serve his reduced sentence, out in five years. But not before he was thoroughly questioned. Jackson Boyd made sure that Mitch got everything he could in return for extreme leniency for a man that Boyd knew would kill again as soon as he got out of prison, if not before.

"Good morning, Mr. Hsiao, or should I just call you Little Pig," Mitch began the interrogation.

Hsiao Tzu was a short skinny Chinese man in his fifties. He had thin greasy hair and a big mole on his cheek with a single black hair poking out of it. The Chinese considered these moles a sign of good luck, and Hsiao Tzu would need all the luck he could get. He wore thick glasses and had bad posture, which made him look as though he was permanently cowering. Mitchell Landau, even with his five-foot-ten-inch frame towered over this man.

"I don't understand why I am here," answered the Little Pig with a thick accent, "I have laundry. I don't know what you want."

"Oh, I think you do, Mr. Hsiao," Mitch continued, "Why don't we play a little game. I will say the names of some very unsavory characters, and you tell me whether you have ever done their laundry. And remember, Mr. Hsiao, as we speak, my men are going over all those receipts we confiscated. If we uncover anything interesting, and I am sure we will, tomorrow we will serve a search warrant on all your other business facilities and your home. If you cooperate, the worst that will happen to you is that the IRS may take some interest in your business activities, and I will make sure that the district attorney's office treats you real nice.

"On the other hand, if you don't give us what we want, and don't be fooled, Mr. Hsiao, we already have the information, we're just looking for corroboration, well then, I will personally see to it that you supervise the laundry facilities in prison for the rest of your life. Do we understand each other, Mr. Hsiao?"

"Am I under arrest? If I am under arrest, I should call my lawyer." The Little Pig stated with uncertainty as his brow was glistening with sweat.

"No, you are not under arrest right now. Are you trying to tell us that we should arrest you? Of course, if that is what you would like, we'll be happy to accommodate you, and you can call any lawyer you'd like. In fact, I can give you the name of a very good lawyer, the same one that Chan Ling had when he was being tried for murder." Mitch saw Hsiao raise his eyes at the mention of Chan Ling.

"Now, I can't tell you a lot of details about Chan Ling's case, but I can tell you that he is on his way to prison to serve a five-year sentence for murder. And if that sounds like a real short time for killing someone in cold blood, think of how short a time you can serve for money laundering. After all, you didn't kill anyone that we know of, or did you, Mr. Hsiao?"

"No, I don't kill no one. I just do laundry. You see, you take me from laundry. I just do laundry." Hsiao was visibly nervous, and Mitch could see his "bean counter" brain calculating the next move.

"Well then, Mr. Hsiao, if you did not kill anyone, you should have nothing to worry about. Now, shall we play our little game, or do you still want your lawyer?" Mitch walked over to the side of the room where Hsiao was sitting, sat on the edge of the table right next to him and turned on the tape recorder.

The First Sign

In her office, Tess was flipping the pages of her desk calendar. Charlie had been gone now for more than three weeks. He'd been a welcome distraction, and she needed him to return. She considered flying to Oregon to surprise him. He could work during the day at the site. She would use the hotel room to do her business. At the end of the day, they would order room service and screw their brains out until the next morning.

But then, she did not even know where he was staying. He said he would call when he got back, and she was not one to push herself, especially when the sole point of the relationship was to soak up from it only what each of them needed. The whole thing would be ruined if either one sought more than the other was willing to give. That was, after all, the beauty of this dance.

Sylvia walked in carrying a cup of tea with milk and a note pad. She placed the tea in front of her boss and sat down in the chair in front of Tess's rosewood desk. When Sylvia first came in for an interview, Tess's initial reaction was that she was too old, too prim, and too stiff to work for her. Now she didn't know what she would do without her. She tried for months to get her to call her Tess, to no avail. Some things were just proper, according to Sylvia, and that was that.

"I am paying bills." Sylvia said. "This bill from First National Bank for the second on your house, is that to be paid from your business or personal account?"

"It should be paid from the same account into which the interest payments from Stone Enterprises are deposited."

"I have not seen any such checks come in." Sylvia said. It was her job to go through the mail and to trouble Tess only with that which required her personal attention. "But I'll keep my eyes peeled." Sylvia jotted a note in her note pad and left.

Walking up to her home that used to house her father and her, Milly Aaron grabbed the stack of mail from the mailbox and dropped it on the table in the foyer. She went through it carefully, but found nothing from Stone Enterprises. It had been three weeks since she was supposed to receive her next payment. She got one interest check when she first signed up, and another two weeks later. A check every two weeks. That was the way this deal was explained to her. She was going to call Jim, but thought better of it. If she was going to take over his restaurant when he retired, she needed to do things on her own.

She found the piece of paper given to her by Charlie Parks with the three names and numbers. She may have been young and inexperienced in these matters, but she would not have invested without references. She never questioned her father's decision to keep the money in trust until she was twenty-five. But she would not have wanted him to question her decisions after she was given the money. The references had all checked out. They had previous experiences with this company and had all received large returns on their investments.

She decided to call Howard Barnes to see if he received his check. She dialed the number on the piece of paper. But instead of Barnes, she got a taped message that the number had been disconnected with no forwarding number. She called information and was told that there was no listing for a Howard Barnes. She called the other two numbers on the list, and got the same results.

As Milly hung up the phone, a terrible feeling came over her. That all the money that Samuel Aaron left her was gone. The money that Milly wanted to use to buy into The Gallery when Jim was ready to retire. Milly stood motionless by the phone, afraid that any move she made would confirm that her fear was a reality. She had no choice. She had to tell Jim.

Jim Pane was on the phone with his CPA.

"Why didn't you tell me this sooner?" Jim asked irritated at his accountant.

"Look, we are a big operation. I thought the checks came in, but were being processed." Answered Martin Hirsch. "I can call and inquire about the delay."

"Forget it," Jim said. "I'll call myself."

Jim hung up and immediately called the number on Charlie Parks's business card.

"This is Charlie. I am sorry I cannot take your call personally . . ." said the prerecorded voice.

"Tess. I have a terrible feeling." Jim said as soon as Tess picked up the phone in her office. "Milly and I have not received our checks from The Oregon Project investment and we cannot get ahold of any of these people. We tried calling the references on the list, but their numbers are disconnected. I can't believe this. I got you and Milly both into this. If this thing goes South, I promise, I will make it up to both of you. I feel awful."

"Jim. Hold on. I am sure there is a perfectly good explanation. Don't jump to conclusions. We have all the paperwork, and I just don't think there is a problem." Tess stopped short of assuring Jim by revealing her relationship with Charlie. "I will check it out and call you back."

Tess left the office, and headed to Century Escrow. She decided that a personal visit would be more productive and, after all, if anything was wrong, it was a lot easier to gauge that in person.

Tess parked her car in that same parking lot where she ran into Charlie and that short balding guy, Walter Manning, which reminded Tess that they had the name of another person to try to reach to see if he had any information that might be helpful. She walked up to the front door of Century Escrow and was relieved to see that it was open for business. Not only that, but the same receptionist was at the front counter.

"Good morning. May I help you," Linda Sanders greeted Tess.

"Good morning. I don't know if you remember me, but I was in here about a month ago to sign paperwork with Mr. Parks for the purchase of The Oregon Project properties. I was wondering if you knew how to get in touch with Mr. Parks in Oregon. There is a problem with our investment checks, and . . ."

"I am sorry, ma'am. I don't seem to recall your being here, and I am afraid I don't know anyone named Charlie Parks. Are you sure you have the right office? You know, there are a lot of escrow companies on this street."

"Yes. I am positive I have the right office, and I am positive that I saw you before." Tess looked around the front lobby. It looked nothing like it did when she was here to sign the escrow papers. Everything from the furniture to the paintings on the wall was different. The only thing that looked the same was Linda, the receptionist, and Tess was sure about that.

"Look, miss." Tess continued. "I am not mistaken about the place or the person I saw here. Would you please tell the owner of this establishment that I need to speak with him or her. I think that will clear a lot of things up."

"Fine," said Linda dialing an extension on her phone. "Mr. Wilson. There is a lady here who would like to speak with you. She is looking for a Mr. Parks and insists that she has been here before to sign escrow documents on some property in Oregon. Yes. All right." Linda hung up the phone. "Mr. Wilson will be right out. Would you please have a seat."

"No, thank you. I will stand." Tess said.

A well dressed African-American man in his late forties came out into the lobby and introduced himself as Kevin Wilson.

"Could we talk in your office, Mr. Wilson?" Tess insisted.

"Certainly. Please come on in." Wilson replied without any hint of concern, and motioned down to the hall towards his office.

As she walked into Wilson's office, Tess could not believe her eyes. This was the same office where she signed the paperwork and handed over the check for $100,000. But the office furniture was different, and there was something else missing, although Tess could not quite figure it out. Oh yes. There was a mirror on this wall which has been replaced by tacky framed poster art. Tess hated poster art.

"Now, how can I help you?" Wilson asked still wearing that saccharin friendly smile.

"My name is Tess Lowe. Three weeks ago," Tess explained, "I sat in this very office, Mr. Wilson, and discussed the purchase of real estate in Oregon with a Charlie Parks. As part of our investment, all investors were to receive monthly checks. Our checks stopped coming, and Mr. Parks told me before he left that he would be in Oregon supervising the completion of this real estate project. I need to get ahold of him to make sure that everything is all right."

"You must be mistaken, Ms. Lowe," Wilson replied. "This has always been my office. We are a very small operation, just Ms. Sanders and myself basically. I do hire overflow help occasionally, but I would certainly know if someone used my office to conduct business. I can assure you that no Charlie Parks worked here. I also don't recall doing any escrows for properties in Oregon. Our escrows are limited to California.

"I wish I could help you, but I believe you must simply be mistaken about the office. Maybe you went to Centurion Escrow—that must be it—it's just down the street, and people frequently confuse us." Wilson stood up and took one of his cards from the business card holder on his desk. "Now, if there is anything else I can do for you, please call me, and I am sorry that I could not help you."

Tess stood up to leave and put the business card in her purse. She felt like she was in the middle of a Twilight Zone episode. But she knew this was the place. It was not Centurion Escrow down the street. And this was the same receptionist. Besides, she had checked copies of the paperwork before coming here and the escrow instructions were on Century Escrow stationery with this address.

Tess decided to check out Charlie's apartment in Brentwood on a remote chance that Charlie would be there. Maybe he lied about the trip to Oregon because he was simply done with their affair. Plenty good. But they also did business, and there was a business problem she had to address sooner rather than later.

The security guard on duty downstairs wore a name tag that said "Carlos" and was more than willing to assist a beautiful woman.

"Mr. Parks doesn't live here anymore." He offered. "In fact, we have a new tenant moving into number 907 this weekend. I think he was moving to Oregon—some real estate thing." Carlos explained.

"What about all his furniture?" Tess asked impatiently.

"Oh, some truck come by a couple days ago and took it somewhere, I don't know. But he doesn't live here anymore, I can tell you that."

"Do you remember the name on the truck?"

"Oh sure. I write everything down—it's my job." Carlos picked up the clipboard from underneath his counter and flipped a few pages. "See. I told you. I write everything down. The name was 'Italian Furniture Rentals,' and the driver who went into the apartment was named 'Ted.' See, he signed right here." Carlos proudly displayed the log entry.

"Carlos, do you have a phone book here, by chance?" Tess asked.

"Sure, here. Is there a problem? Maybe I can help." Carlos volunteered as he put the Yellow Pages on the counter.

"Oh, no thank you," Tess said, "you've been very helpful."

CHAPTER

Cancun

Charlie finished another cigarette and bottomed off the Mai Tai with a one thirsty gulp. The hot Mexican sun turned his already dark skin into golden brown. He had been in Cancun for two weeks. Drinking and tanning. Charlie's share of Tess's investment was deposited into his bank account as promised.

He made a lot of money from The Oregon Project which should last him for a while. But, as was his custom and practice, it was burning a hole in Charlie's pocket, and he felt as though he wanted to spend every last dime. The joy of money was in making it and spending it. Having too much at any one time actually made Charlie nervous. There was something very unfamiliar and troubling about it.

Charlie's father was one of those men who believed that children should be seen and not heard. His mother had little time for Charlie or his sister. It was her responsibility to keep food on the table since his father was either too drunk to go to work or passed out in some other woman's bed. When his mother was not working, she spent her time fending off her husband, who took out the frustration over his miserable existence on her.

Starving for attention, Charlie was constantly stirring up trouble, but since neither his mother nor father had any time or desire to parent, their motto was "Boys will be boys." By the time he reached high school, Charlie had caught the eye of most of the girls. They found his disheveled appearance and "bad boy" attitude appealing. Most of his friends were trying drugs, everything from marijuana to LSD to heroine. Charlie didn't. His drug of choice was getting away with things. There was a certain thrill in that, and the risks were acceptable, especially growing up in a family where discipline and punishment were not part of the regimen.

It was hard to spend a lot of money in any one place without getting bored. So Charlie traveled from place to place in Mexico until George would give him permission to come back to the United States. That was the arrangement, and Charlie did not question it. He checked in with George once a week at a preset time. When George felt comfortable that their tracks were covered, he would give Charlie the O.K. to return and they would decide where he should live and what he would do next.

Before Charlie left for Mexico, George told him that he took $10,000 from Charlie's share and gave it to the Bellinger campaign. Although this decision was made unilaterally by George, Charlie thought this was a small price to pay for the district attorney to look the other way. Besides, Charlie was sure that George's personal contribution was much larger.

As the sun set into the clear blue Caribbean water, Charlie picked up his cigarettes and suntan lotion and walked into the Krystal Hotel. He opened the door to his suite overlooking the ocean and noticed that the red button on the phone was lit. Something must have gone wrong. The only person who knew that he was here was George, and Charlie was not scheduled to speak with him until Thursday, two days from now. He called the front desk and got the message that Walter Manning called and was expecting a return phone call tonight at 9:00 PM California time. Charlie and George began using Walter Manning as George's alias ever since that run-in with Tess in the parking lot of Century Escrow.

At 9:00 PM sharp, the phone rang in George Stone's study.

"Hello, golden boy," George greeted Charlie.

"Is my prison term over, warden. Am I being released for good behavior?"

"That all depends."

"On what?"

"On whether your girlfriend gets off our tails." George snapped.

"What are you talking about, George. What's going on?"

"I told you, you can't fuck the same person you steal from. Your girlfriend has been asking questions at Century Escrow about you. Lucky for us, Wilson and the receptionist fended her off. It's amazing what $5,000 and a trip to Hawaii will do. Wilson will keep his mouth shut. That all-paid vacation he took to Hawaii during the time we took over Century Escrow was with his mistress. He told his wife and kids that he was going away on business. We've got pictures and Wilson knows it. Sanders is another story. She probably already snorted her share of the money and may be asking for more. But even so, her only contact was with a Charlie Parks who no longer exists. If she tries to reach you, she'll get nowhere. I've got a man watching them. If the trail stops there, we're O.K."

"When am I coming home? I mean, Mexico is nice, but I am getting tired of drinking bottled water."

"I'm getting to that. I have a new project for you. It's in New Orleans. I'll give you the details when I see you, but it should be right up your alley. It has to do with cars. Tomorrow night at 10:00 PM your time, be at the El Capitan bar. My man will find you and give you everything you need."

"I'm not sure New Orleans is such a good idea for me, George. I've been there."

"You can give me all your objections when I see you. Meanwhile, in a show of good faith, there is an extra $20,000 in your account. An advance, shall we say, to encourage you not to object too strenuously to this next project. You're perfect for it, Charlie. The Oregon Project will seem like small potatoes when you're done with this one. By the way, there's one more thing. It's probably nothing to worry about. But remember Hsiao Tzu, the guy you met at Bellinger's bash?"

"Yeah, the Little Pig who did laundry."

"That's him. The cops picked him up and searched his business. I don't know what's going on, but I don't think he'll squeal. His customers include people much scarier than I am."

"Have you looked in the mirror lately, George. 'Scary' is not exactly the word I'd use for you."

"I'll see you soon, Charlie." George hung up.

Charlie quickly dialed the international operator to check on his bank balance. George was a man of his word. The account was indeed $20,000 richer, and so was Charlie.

Italian Furniture Rentals

Italian Furniture Rentals, Inc., despite its fancy name, was located in a seedy part of town near Venice Beach. A couple blocks back, Tess stopped her car and put the top up on her Mustang convertible. It was no longer safe to drive with the top down. She locked the doors and turned on the air conditioning.

When she entered the store, the showroom was filled with leather couches, love seats, glass tables, and bedroom sets. Tess recognized the couch that was in Charlie's apartment and the bed on which they first made love. It was obvious that Charlie did more than go to Oregon on a business trip, or made up a story to end a short affair. He was gone. And while the personal side of this was only minimally troubling to Tess, she was beginning to believe that Jim Pane's concerns about their investments were well taken.

"Looking for anything in particular?" Asked a salesman.

"Yes. I need to speak with Ted. I understand that he drives one of your delivery trucks." Tess explained.

"Ted, Ted," the salesman mumbled thoughtfully. "If he drives one of our trucks, he will be in the warehouse. Go out that door and turn to your right. Be careful with the stairs."

Tess thanked the man and followed his directions. She found the warehouse filled with furniture, but no people. Through the open rear door, she noticed a truck with "Italian Furniture Rentals" written on the side. A large unshaven man wearing grungy green overalls closed the gate of the truck and stepped into the cab, but had not yet shut the door.

"Excuse me," Tess yelled out. "Excuse me. Are you Ted?"

"That's me." The man yelled back from the cab. "But if there is a problem with your delivery, you gotta talk to the manager inside the store."

"No, no problem with the delivery." Tess caught up to Ted and stood at the side of the cab. "I just need to ask you a couple of questions, if you don't mind."

Ted turned off the engine and stepped out of the truck. He leaned against the driver's door and put his hands in the pockets of his overalls.

"What do you wanna ask me?"

"You picked up some furniture from the Brentwood Luxury Apartments a couple weeks ago. The security guard gave me your name. I am looking for Charlie Parks, the man whose furniture you picked up there. Do you have any information on where he might be?"

"Why you wanna know? If he didn't tell you, why would he tell me?"

Tess determined that the business explanation might smack of more involvement than any stranger would want to undertake or even listen to.

"It's personal . . . I wish I could tell you, but I would be too embarrassed." Tess was hoping Ted would assume that it was something of a female nature, like she was pregnant, and not persist with his uestions. But, in all honestly, she was embarrassed. She was guessing now that she was taken by the man her instincts told her to distrust. Ironically, while she was busy using him to squelch her own loneliness, her own desire for company and distraction, he used her for something more sinister. The sex was mutual, the con, if that's what it was, was not.

Ted put his hands deeper into his pockets and stared at his shoes. He debated for a minute about whether to help this woman. He'd been turned down by enough good looking girls when he was younger so that he stopped asking them out and has, since then, harbored a strong resentment towards women in general. But he hated men who mistreated beautiful women more. He would treat them right. It's too bad that they never gave him the chance to prove it.

"All I know is what I overheard. I never talked to this guy Parks. I heard the boss saying that this guy had a large deposit, and something about a P.O. box or something to mail it to after we pick up the furniture."

"Did you hear where this P.O. box was?" Tess asked.

"Nah, that's all I know," Ted said getting back into his truck. "My boss, Mel, he's inside the office now. He should know." Ted started the engine again and took off the emergency brake.

Mel was inside his office with the door open adding up receipts and chewing on an unlit cigar. Tess stepped in and waited to be acknowledged. Mel knew that someone came into his office but did not lift his head from the receipts or the calculator which he was using with a high degree of skill:

"Yeah."

"Hi . . . Are you Mel?" Tess asked.

Mel looked up and smiled. "Yeah, I'm Mel. I am the owner of this store. You need furniture to rent. I will make you a deal on anything you see. And if you don't see what you like, I'll get you what you like."

"Actually, Mel, I need your assistance on a personal matter. May I close the door?" The story worked once.

"What kind of personal matter? Please sit down." He motioned for Tess to sit down, walked over to the front of the desk and sat on the edge.

"My name is Tess Lowe."

Mel stared at Tess as if approving that the name fit her looks.

"I understand that a man by the name of Charlie Parks rented some furniture from you, and that you might know where he is. You see, I have a personal problem with which Mr. Parks left me . . . and I need to tell him about it as soon as possible."

Mel smiled so wide that his cigar almost fell out of his mouth. For an instant he imagined how Tess got this personal problem. He had a vivid imagination fueled by years of watching pornographic movies. He walked back behind his desk and sat down. He reached for a lighter, slowly lit his cigar, leaned back in his chair and planted his legs on the desk. The smell of the cigar almost made Tess gag.

"Let me get this straight. You got knocked up, excuse me, you got a personal problem, and you want me to give you where this Mr. Parks is so that you can tell him about it. Do I have this right?"

"Mel. I understand that you have the location of the P.O. box where he is. That's all I need. It's very important. Please." Tess said.

"Look, lady, this chap was a customer—a good customer—I don't think your problem is any of my business. I figure if he wanted you to know where he was, he'd send you a postcard. Besides, he told me he would call me with the address of the P.O. box, and I haven't heard from him yet. See, I ain't too anxious to hear from him, cause the deal was if he doesn't call me for thirty days with the address, I can keep the deposit. Two grand is a good chunk of change. So, you see, I figure a man that generous deserves a little privacy."

"So, what you're saying is that if and when he calls, you still won't give me the information."

"Yeah, that's what I'm saying. It just ain't any of my business to get involved in that kind of a problem. Now," Mel continued chewing on his cigar, "if you'd like some furniture to rent, I'll be happy to accommodate you."

Tess realized she'd reached a dead end. She called Jim Pane from her car and shared with him the events of the day.

"I think we should call the police." Jim said.

"Jim, they don't even look for missing persons until they've been gone for forty-eight hours." Tess disagreed. "Besides, what are we going to tell them. The paperwork shows that we all own real estate in Oregon for which we paid. The only thing missing are some interest payments."

Tess could hear the cops now.

"Sure, ma'am. We will devote not one but two officers to pursue your overstuffed investment, while we barely scrape to make ends meet on our salaries."

Portland, Oregon

The next morning, Tess boarded the first flight out to Portland, Oregon, the location of her four vacant lots. She thought of asking Jim to go with her, but decided against it. If Charlie was there, they had a lot to discuss.

The plane landed right on time. Sylvia booked her return flight for 8:00 PM that evening. This would give Tess plenty of time to get to the site of the project, to ask questions and to get back to the airport. That is, assuming that she did not run into Charlie.

Tess picked up her rental car, a map, and headed North on the freeway. The clerk at Enterprise Rent-a-Car told her that it should take her about an hour to get to the general location. The drive was pretty and gave her time to think. She ran everything through her mind. The first meeting with Charlie, Jim's recommendation, the three investors on the list that Charlie gave her. A certain calm came over her. A clarity that she was glad to see arrive. This was all one big overreaction, she analyzed.

Charlie was a mistake, she had to admit. Despite the pleasurable frivolity of the moment, she deserved more respect and did not appreciate being lied to. But now, Charlie would be relegated to another one of those life episodes from which you learned and which, later in life, you could fit perfectly into that reserved piece of your life's puzzle. Nothing more.

The interest checks were obviously a gimmick, but so what. The ultimate financial loss was not that great. It was a come-on to sell the properties, no different than a bank inviting you to borrow with no points only to charge you some made up administrative fee when you commit to the loan. The ultimate buy-out was also a lie, unless Takushi was real. But, again, what they've lost is the "too good to be true" return on their investment, not their investment.

The bottom line was that they owned property in Oregon. It was not exactly what any of them wanted, but it had value. They would simply sell it, recover what they could, and if there were any differ- ence, write it off on their taxes. They certainly lost no more than people lose in the stock market, and no one faults them for taking those risks. It was all clear now, and she would not let her affair with Charlie cloud her judgment.

Tess took the off ramp, and headed north on the street paralleling the freeway. According to the map, this road would soon turn into a large size lot with vacant parcels. Tess passed several ranch style homes. It was a nice area. She could totally see a self-contained development going up here. A school, a theater, a gym. She was looking for 4598 through 4664 Dew Road. Anything close to that would do. She was on the right road, but it became harder to spot the addresses.

Tess saw a man getting into his pickup truck in front of one of the homes and stopped. She stepped out of her rental car and said,

"Excuse me, sir."

The man turned around and quizzically lifted his head.

"I'm sorry to trouble you, but I am looking for some undeveloped lots, numbers 4598 through 4664 Dew Road."

The man closed his car door and walked up to her.

"I'm sorry," he said. "What are the numbers you are looking for?"

"4598 through 4664," Tess repeated.

"Are you sure it's Dew Road that you want?" The man asked. "Because there are no such numbers on this street. My house is 1275 and the last place on this road is 1688. After that, the street ends and you run into some army barracks."

"Is there another Dew Road? Maybe I'm mistaken." Tess was hoping.

"Not that I know of. Not in this town."

"Thank you." Tess said and walked back to her car.

She drove to the end of Dew Road. She made a U-turn and drove to the other end. She drove around the neighborhood for good measure. On the way back to the airport, she stopped by the Chamber of Commerce. She inquired of the very polite lady at the front desk if she perhaps took a wrong turn. There was only one Dew Road in this town, she was told. But just to be on the safe side, the lady checked on the computer and apologized that she could not deliver better news.

The calm that characterized her state of being just hours before was a distant memory.

Tommy

Tommy Simon worked for the large insurance defense firm of Megan and Potters. The firm had ten partners, fifty lawyers, and took up two floors of a ten-story office building in Beverly Hills. Tommy's office was on the sixth floor. He had been defending insurance companies, or more accurately, their insured clients, for twelve years and could not recall one year when he enjoyed it. He had heard every type of possible scenario for car crashes and slip and falls.

After the first two years, he stopped caring about who was right. He worked up the case with as many billable hours as possible and then recommended settlement to his clients. He used to want to try cases where he thought his client was in the right, but the firm's policy was to avoid trials at all costs. With few major clients paying the tab for the entire firm, one bad loss at trial could mean the loss of that client, and with it, thousands of dollars each month. Tommy resented this policy, and resented everything about this practice, but he was earning $180,000 per year plus bonus, and that money afforded him a lifestyle that he thoroughly enjoyed—a house on the beach and yearly trips anywhere in the world. He loved to travel. It put things in perspective.

Tommy was in the middle of a deposition. The plaintiff who pretended not to speak any English and requested a Spanish interpreter was describing how he slipped on a piece of lettuce at a local market. Once in a while, the plaintiff would forget about the interpreter and answer the question in English, at which point Tommy would methodically make a record that the witness appeared to have understood his question in English without the necessity of a translation.

Frankly, Tommy could not care less about making a detailed record. This was routine. After the deposition, Tommy would get authorization from the insurance adjuster to offer to pay the plaintiff's medical bills which miraculously have mounted to $4,250.00 for a simple fall on the butt, which offer would be readily accepted. The plaintiff's attorney would take one-third of this amount as a fee for doing a few hours of work, the medical bills would be reduced to one-third of their stated amount, which was probably already prenegotiated between the lawyer and the medical facility, and Mr. Fernandez, the "injured" party, would likewise recover one-third of the offer for falling on his rear end, if that's in fact what happened.

Tommy never ceased to be amazed at how insurance adjusters rationalized paying medical bills on these worthless cases and yet fought him on every dollar of those cases where the defendant was clearly at fault and the plaintiff was clearly and seriously injured. He concluded the deposition with the usual stipulation relieving the court reporter of her responsibilities of maintaining the original transcript, shook hands with plaintiff's counsel, picked up his file and walked out of the conference room.

He walked through the lobby and headed to his office at the end of the hall. He was not tall for a man, but made up for lack of height with broad shoulders and a muscular build. His hair was prematurely grey, but it detracted nothing from his young appearance and appealing manner.

After slaving for this firm for ten years, he had finally gotten the coveted corner office. He had also been offered partnership, but declined. It was a move that shocked all the lawyers in the firm. But he knew it was the right move. To be a partner meant that he had to pay the firm $90,000 for the privilege while risking a decline in his income if the firm had a bad year. Partnership did not mean that his name would be added to the firm's name, as it was destined to remain Megan and Potters forever. Plus, as a partner, he ran the risk of incurring personal liability for the acts of the other partners whom he knew well enough not to want to be responsible for, and whom he disliked enough to decide otherwise.

Tess had been waiting patiently in the lobby. Tommy's secretary offered to interrupt Tommy in the deposition because of her familiarity with Tess, but Tess declined. Her relationship with Tommy was over. She did not feel right about interrupting him while he worked. For the three years that they were together, Tommy insisted on helping Tess with all her legal matters. He drafted her contracts and reviewed those offered to her. He even helped her with the lawsuit she had to file to collect money from one gallery owner who sold an artwork and refused to pay Tess her rightful share. As much as he hated practicing law, he loved knowing that he could help Tess. He refused to charge for his legal services, and Tess insisted on making it up to him by taking him to dinners.

When Tess finally collected from the restaurant owner, she paid for their ski trip to Canada for a week. At first, Tommy resisted the idea of Tess paying for the entire trip, but Tess insisted that it cost her substantially less than if she had to pay reasonable attorney's fees. Besides, if he refused, she would never allow him to help her again.

That was then. Now, Tess was sitting in the same lobby where she often met Tommy for lunch, and felt like a complete stranger.

"Tess," Tommy exclaimed with surprise as he walked into the lobby and saw the only woman he ever truly loved.

"I know I should have called."

"No, that's fine. Come on, let's go to my office. Do you want something to drink?"

"Water would be fine." Tommy escorted Tess into his office and requested water through the intercom.

"How have you been?" Tommy asked gently.

"Tommy, I'm sorry, but I did not come here for personal reasons." Tess wanted to make sure that her intentions were clear immediately. After all, he walked out on her. "I am here because I don't know where else to turn. It's a serious problem that involves not only me, but Jim Pane and his niece, Milly, and I am sure other people too. Do you have the time to hear me out?"

"Of course." Tommy answered.

The secretary brought in a glass of water for Tess and closed the door on the way out. Tommy listened intently as Tess described The Oregon Project, Charlie Parks, and the investments. She relayed everything except her involvement with Charlie. It was not relevant, she reasoned. And besides, it was none of his business. He could not possibly have been alone during this entire year that they have been apart.

"Have you called the police?" Tommy asked.

"No. I don't see why they would get interested in this. Besides, what do I tell them? That they should put aside their murder and rape cases to help me when I was stupid enough to get conned?"

"Well, we can file a lawsuit against Charlie Parks and Stone Enterprises. If we can't find him, we'll serve the lawsuit on him by publication—it's just a formality—and get a default judgment against him for the full amount of your loss. That way, if he ever appears, we can try and attach his assets."

"Tommy, this guy is a professional. I appreciate the suggestion, but I think a lawsuit is just going to be a waste of time and money."

"You know I wouldn't charge you."

"Unacceptable. I refuse to allow you to do any legal work for me for free. Besides, I am not here to ask you to sue Charlie Parks. Frankly, I'm not sure why I'm here. I guess I am desperately looking for suggestions."

"Look, Tess. Leave the file with me. Let me make some calls and see what I can find out. You know that if I can do anything to help you, I will. I still care about you."

"Tommy. Don't." Tess said. She was afraid that everything that had happened combined with seeing Tommy again would cause her to break down. She did not cry easily. It was a sign of weakness, and she considered herself to be one of the strongest people she knew. That's why it burned so much that, in a weak moment, she let herself be fooled by one man and now had to turn to the man who left her for help.

"I'm sorry. I tried to explain." Tommy said. "I just wasn't ready for us, for marriage. But I'm not the one who wanted to stop all contact and communication."

"No, Tommy, you just wanted to keep going on forever, in some glorified boyfriend and girlfriend routine. I'm thirty-two years old, Tommy. I want children. I grew up in a family of ten.

I was very honest with you about that when we started to get serious. I wanted them with you." Tess said.

"Tess, I just wanted some more time."

"You left me, Tommy." Tess brought the subject into focus.

"You gave me an ultimatum. I didn't want you completely out of my life, but out of the two choices . . ."

The two fell silent. They were revisiting a conversation that they had rehearsed so many times before, with lines so often repeated that they were all but memorized. They both knew where it would lead and how it would end.

Tess got up to leave.

"Anything you can do, Tommy, please let me know. I feel awful about being scammed, and I feel terrible about asking for your help."

"Tess, I was just going to get something to eat. Can I take you to lunch?" Tommy prodded tentatively.

"Tommy, look. I just need some legal help. Please, it was difficult enough to come here."

"O.K. I understand. I'll look at this and call you tomorrow. Are you still at the same number?"

"Yes. I haven't moved."

Tess left the Megan and Potters building, and headed to her office. She began to question why she went to see Tommy. The man was a civil attorney and yet she knew that a lawsuit is not what she wanted. Now that she allowed herself the freedom of honesty, she knew why she went to see Tommy. She succumbed to the overwhelming lingering desire to see him. The Oregon Project fiasco gave her a legitimate excuse.

El Capitan

The El Capitan bar in the Zona Hotelera in Cancun, Mexico was crowded with tourists wearing shorts and tank tops. They drank shots of tequila, and chased it with Modelo, the local beer. The D.J. played American pop music of the 1950s and '60s, and a couple who obviously had too much to drink was dancing on a small dance floor to the appropriately chosen rendition of "Tequila."

Charlie proceeded to the bar where he sat down on a stool and ordered a Dos Equis. For a moment, he let himself think of Tess and imagined them as regular people vacationing in Mexico, drinking beer and dancing. A man Charlie assumed was a tourist since he was dressed the part, got up off a bar stool at the end of the bar and sat next to Charlie. He introduced himself as John and asked Charlie to move to a small table at the corner of the room. Charlie grabbed his beer and followed the stranger.

When they sat down, the man handed Charlie an envelope and said, "This has a new passport, driver's license, etc. You are flying out tomorrow to Miami and then changing flights to New Orleans. The tickets are also in the envelope. In New Orleans, we made reservations for you at the Louisiana Inn. It's a small hotel where you will meet with George on Sunday. After that, you will receive your instructions directly from George. Need anything else?" The man ended his speech.

"No. Looks like it's all covered." Charlie said.

Without saying another word, the man stood up and left.

Charlie finished his beer and proceeded to his hotel room to pack. When he got to his suite, he took out the envelope and tore it open. Next to his picture on the passport and driver's license was the name "Sean Masters."

"How preppy," Charlie thought as he tried to get used to yet another new identity.

Part II

CHAPTER

The Face-Off

The morning after Hsiao Tzu's inquisition, Grant Bellinger and Mitchell Landau met in Bellinger's office. Despite big windows beaming in sunlight, the office appeared dark. On the walls were the usual plaques confirming the contents of Bellinger's curriculum vitae. The University of Wisconsin bestowed on him a bachelor's degree in political science and USC gave him his law degree. Then there were honors, awards, and plaques of appreciation from everyone from Mothers Against Drunk Drivers to the Mayor's Office. In the center of one of the walls was a photograph of Bellinger in uniform during his JAG days next to some military commanders. Mitch wondered how these people would respond to Bellinger hobnobbing with the Chinese mafia.

Bellinger was of two minds about the serious progress that Mitch was making against the Chinese cartel. If Landau was successful in going to the media about his efforts, Bellinger would get an early retirement. The Berardo conviction combined with putting away Chinese mafia hoodlums would be impossible to overcome. However, if Bellinger was successful in taking credit for these arrests, he would be that much closer to winning reelection. Besides, he was running out of tricks in his hat. The polls were now showing the two candidates in a virtual dead heat.

Ike Murdoch had come up with nothing and was called off the job after the fumbled attempt to have Landau picked up for drunk driving. It is too bad that Landau was not driving that night, Bellinger lamented. His people could certainly have gotten some mileage from the incident. Newsome had been advising Bellinger to hold a press conference about these mob arrests. That is, as soon as the arrests were made.

"How do you know that this Hsiao Tzu—or whatever his name is—isn't lying to you just to save his skin." Bellinger asked.

Mitch was not fooled by Bellinger's keen interest in the prospective arrests. He knew the D.A., not the assistant D.A., would get the spotlight, but he did not care. Nothing like setting Bellinger up just to knock him down.

"We have confirmation from his books. He kept records of everyone who brought money in. They are coded, but he swears that once we get the code, we will have the names, dates, and amounts. It's simply a matter of making a deal with this guy."

"Whose names do you think you'll get," Bellinger asked perfunctorily. He already made the decision to proceed.

"If Hsiao is to be believed, at least a dozen upper echelon in one local family and a number of their enforcers as well as some Caucasian white collar criminals. Most of these guys run their business out of Hong Kong and Taipei. But some have settled here. Remember the series of bank robberies, eight or nine of them, two years ago. Two people killed, five wounded, no suspects. The cops swear the Chinese mafia was involved. The composites were all of Asian men. I'm sure that is only the tip of the iceberg. This is big, Grant, I can't believe you would even hesitate to offer this peon a deal."

"I am not hesitating, Landau, I am thinking it through—a difference you will learn after you do this for as many years as I have." Bellinger loved rubbing in their age difference. Besides, he truly believed that it made him a better D.A. "How do you plan to proceed?" He asked.

"We'll offer Hsiao a deal he can't refuse. I'm thinking two years in the pokey plus five years' probation for money laundering. I've talked to Roberts at the IRS. He's agreed that, as long as they get back taxes plus penalties from Hsiao, they'll leave him alone. They figure there's bigger fish to fry with the Chinese we are going to bring in. They are confident that every one of them has a lot of reckoning to do with the IRS. Once Hsiao accepts the deal, he'll decode his books, and we'll get search warrants and arrest warrants."

"You think Hsiao will take the deal?"

"I don't think he is worried about serving the time. He's more worried about getting his head blown off. He'll have to get 'round the clock protection once the arrests are made. And once he gets out of prison, he may ask to go into witness protection. You see any problem with that?" Mitch asked.

"Once we convict the scum he's worked for, I couldn't care less what happens to him." Bellinger responded coolly.

"That's what I figured."

"By the way," Bellinger stopped Mitch at the door. "One thing has me puzzled. You and I both know that I will take credit for this roundup, and it can only help me at the polls. So what's in it for you?"

"Believe it or not, Grant, getting criminals off the street is more important to me than winning the election. Even if it means losing to you."

"Your naïveté never ceases to amaze me." Bellinger said.

"It's not naïveté." Mitch answered poignantly. "It's integrity. Something you know little about."

The Arrests

Two weeks later, at 3:00 AM, a team of thirty LAPD officers with search and arrest warrants was dispatched to numerous homes in the best and worst areas of town. They were met with no resistance. It took time to go through Hsiao Tzu's records, even after he decoded them. And Mitch had to make sure that the warrants were well founded as he wanted no loopholes. Not on this one.

All in all, twelve arrest warrants were issued and, by 4:30 AM, nine arrests had been made. There was no answer at the doors of two other homes, those of Li Ming and Wu Tang. The cops broke into each and confiscated the items on the search warrant and, for good measure, a lot more.

He was sound asleep when he heard a loud bang on his door. He put on his silk robe and slippers and went downstairs. He could see the uniforms through the glass in the front door and paused for a brief moment contemplating his options. There were none. He opened the door.

"Mr. George Stone?" asked the detective wearing a suit and tie. The two uniformed LAPD officers were standing on each side of him as if to protect him from the unarmed Stone.

"Yes. What can I do for you, officers?"

"Mr. Stone. I'm Detective Jack Tatum. We have a warrant for your arrest and a search warrant for your house." Tatum took out the envelope from the inside pocket of his jacket.

George pretended to read the documents although his eyes could not focus. A million thoughts raced through his head, including an extremely illogical thought about trying to escape. Having calculated his options, George stated with a calm that surprised even him:

"These papers appear to be in order, although I have no idea what it is you want with me. What are the charges against me, Detective?"

"They'll explain all that to you downtown, sir. Right now, would you please turn around so that I can place handcuffs on you while my officers confiscate the items listed in the search warrant."

George stepped back into the house allowing the detective and the officers to enter.

"May I put on some clothes?"

Jack motioned to one of the uniformed officers to follow George into his bedroom.

When George returned fully dressed, he walked up to the detective, who was still standing near the doorway, turned around and put his wrists together to allow himself to be handcuffed. He appeared cool and collected, but inside he was petrified. It was this feeling that he feared most in life. It was this feeling that made him act so carefully and meticulously no matter what he did. What went wrong?

As he watched the officers take crates of documents out of his house, he heard the detective read him his rights. The crates were filled with several Rolodex, calendars, and files from the file cabinet. None of that concerned George as the only documents he kept in his house were from legitimate business deals and investments. The only thing George worried about at that moment were the handcuffs on his wrists, which were beginning to cut into his skin and caused shivers up and down his spine.

The ride downtown was quiet. Jack Tatum, an eighteen-year veteran of the force, knew better than to try to interrogate Stone in the car. He knew that if he tried, one of two things would happen. Stone would either tell him to buzz off until he got ahold of his lawyer or give him information and then claim that it was without the benefits of knowing his Miranda rights.

Jack was two years away from retirement. He could stay on the force as long as he wanted, but he was ready for a change. His two sons were grown and self-sufficient. He and his wife Kate looked forward to his retirement and had saved up for and purchased a condo in Palm Desert, just twenty minutes from Palm Springs, which they now visited almost every weekend. It was quiet, peaceful, and safe.

Throughout his career, Jack had had his share of confrontations with the criminal element. After years on the force, he finally admitted to himself that he had rather enjoyed the excitement. But now it was just a job. With only two years left, he and Kate frequently joked about Jack doing as much desk duty as possible, and she would often send him off to work by saying "Try not to get killed. It'll be lonely without you in Palm Springs."

When they arrived downtown, the media hounds were already present in droves, having a field day with every police car. They knew that each man who got out of the car with handcuffs could buy and sell all of them without blinking, and this added to the thrill. Jack marveled at people's fascination with the mafia. These bastards robbed and killed for a living, and yet there has always been a certain level of respect for them. Jack reasoned that it must be because their code of honor was so black and white. You cross me, you die, you pledge allegiance to me, and I'll protect you. Even Jack admitted that there was a certain appeal to these simple rules. Not like the street gangs who killed innocent children because these creeps happened to be bad shots from a distance. "Cowards," Jack thought.

The black and white pulled into the parking lot of the downtown station and stopped. The press was ready for the arrival of the next "gangster" and hovered over the car. George Stone, who had been preoccupied with the decision of which lawyer to retain and how best to get the plea for help to Bellinger, noticed the media circus for the first time.

"What's going on?" George queried as Jack opened the rear door and assisted the arrestee out of the car.

"We're making a lot of busts this morning. Mostly the Chinese mob."

George paused and stared at the cameras and the reporters. "Hsiao Tzu," he mumbled to himself as the realization of the extent of his problems permeated his being.

Jack Tatum led George Stone through the crowd of reporters, accompanied by the two uniformed officers. George wanted to shield his face from the cameras, but he had nothing to do it with as his hands remained handcuffed. He cowered and turned his face from side to side trying to avoid that camera which he thought was focused on him at the time. The reporters were yelling out questions over each other, and it all became one loud hum as he finally found safety behind the walls of the police station.

That morning, Tess was following her usual routine getting ready for work. She found herself more and more preoccupied with solving The Oregon Project riddle. Yes, there was the sting of what she knew now was outright theft, but it was also personal. The only way Charlie Parks got to her money was through her. She was used, in every sense of the word. But all the roads she took, all the clues she followed, led to a hollow end.

The checks the investors had given to Stone Enterprises were cashed through a small bank in San Diego, and the account has since been closed. She had faxed the copy of the deed to the Oregon land to the county recorder's office in Portland. The deed was a confirmed forgery.

Tommy called the secretary of state and ran Stone Enterprises on the Lexis Legal Research website. The corporation came into existence one year ago, and has since been suspended for failure to pay franchise taxes. Another way of saying that whoever formed it had no more use for it, Tommy explained.

"The president is listed as Charlie Parks, whom we still have not been able to locate," Tommy reported during one of their phone calls, "and the agent for service of process is C.T. Corporation in downtown Los Angeles. These guys basically accept service of lawsuits for hundreds of companies. I'm sorry, Tess. I'll keep looking."

Dressed and made up, Tess walked into the kitchen to pour a cup of coffee that had brewed on a preset timer. She turned on Channel 4 and watched the *Today Show* with Katie Couric and Matt Lauer. There was a report on the numerous arrests made in the middle of the night. Tess caught something about the Chinese mafia and turned away to get cream for her coffee from the refrigerator. When she turned back, she stopped in disbelief. There, in the middle of her screen, being led in handcuffs was the short balding guy she knew as

Walter Manning. Tess stared at the screen until Manning disappeared into the police station.

At 8:30 that morning, Grant Bellinger, Mitchell Landau, and Jack Tatum were in Bellinger's office going through the details of that morning's arrests. The press conference was scheduled for 11:00 AM. That would give Bellinger enough time to familiarize himself with all the details to be able to answer the questions from the press and make sure that he made the noon news.

It was agreed that after the general rundown on the carrying out of the arrests and search warrants, the individual cases would be presented to Bellinger alphabetically. Jack described that the arrests were accomplished without incident, that they only had to break into two homes because the suspects were not present. The loot confiscated was quite impressive. Jack reported that there must have been at least $200,000 in cash, thirty or forty weapons, and probably forty kilos of cocaine. He did not have all the exact figures, but the inventory should be finished before 11:00 AM and certainly in time for the press conference. After the inventory was completed, the loot would be placed in the big conference room for display to the press.

When Jack was finished, Mitch picked up from the stack on the floor the first file alphabetically.

"Bao Tsing. We've seen this guy before. His rap sheet is quite a sight. He ran a whorehouse in Hong Kong, but then decided to branch out in California. He was busted twice, once for pimping and the other time for narcotics. Plea bargained the first one with no time, just probation, and was acquitted on the second. Jackson Boyd was his lawyer and got him off. The jury decided that there wasn't enough evidence that Bao was the guy who committed the crime. He got our star witness to admit that all Orientals looked the same to him."

"Sounds like a real charmer." Bellinger remarked leaning back comfortably in his chair.

"Da Matzu. Good news. Fellenzer with the FBI thinks he recognized this guy as matching the composite drawing of one of the bank robbers. They're pulling the file and checking the computers on him. If he matches the composite, they'll get ahold of the bank people and do a lineup. We may have gotten one of them."

"Jack, let's try to get the composite before 11:00. I'd love to be able to tell the people of L.A., who suffered through those bank robberies, that we nabbed one of the bastards."

"I bet you would," Mitch thought.

"All right. I'll get with Fellenzer as soon as we're done with the booking." Jack responded.

Mitch continued with the presentation on each of the files until he got to the last one alphabetically, and his favorite one.

"George Stone. This guy doesn't seem to fit the mold of Hsiao's customers, but he did use him for money laundering. It's confirmed in Hsiao's books. This is one of those Caucasian white collar criminals I was telling you we could anticipate to get from Hsiao's records."

"Aha." Bellinger froze in his seat. This could not be happening. Not George. Why the hell didn't he check the arrest warrants before they went out. Now it was too late. He had to get to George before this went any further—or before the unimaginable happened and George talked. But how? How does he insist on treating this guy differently without giving it away?

"We haven't yet gone through all the stuff we confiscated from his house. But for the most part, there's nothing there. So far, he's charged with tax evasion. Hsiao says this guy has been running illegal schemes for years and has been Hsiao's customer for five of those years. Once we learn more about Stone's dealings, with Hsiao's testimony, we can probably also charge him with criminal fraud. I've got a call into Roberts. We may want IRS's help on this one."

"All right." Bellinger said attempting to keep his voice on an even keel. "Where are these guys now?"

"We put the most hardened ones in the cells. Some of them, including this guy Stone are still sitting in the interrogation rooms waiting to be processed." Jack Tatum explained.

"You've done well." Bellinger said staring at the wall and not directing his comment to either man in particular. "There is one more thing I'd like to do before the press conference. I want to see the arrestees themselves—you know—get a feel for the criminal element we've busted. I think it will help me explain things better to the press. Jack, you can guide me to the cells and tell me who's who, and let me see the stash you collected. I can do the interrogation rooms myself while you get on top of this composite situation. Mitch, you're due in court on the Stuttz arraignment, aren't you?"

"Yes. The arraignment was set for 8:30 AM, but I got ahold of Judge Spencer and told her about the excitement here. She said she'd hold it 'till 9:00 o'clock if we promised not to have all these matters go to trial at the same time. Says her calendar is crazy as it is. Anyway, I better go. I should be back by 10:00 and we can go over any loose ends then before the big conference."

Interrogation Room 4

George Stone felt himself shivering as his white silk shirt was drenched with sweat and was now clinging to his body. He did not know whether he was shivering from fear or from the cold air pumped into the interrogation room from the overworked air conditioner. Nor did he care. He had been in that room for more than three hours now. He asked to call a lawyer, and was told that he would get his chance as soon as he was processed. But due to the sheer number of the arrests made that morning, he would just have to wait. Besides, he was told, he should be grateful that he is in an interrogation room and not in one of the cells. George had to admit that he was grateful for that.

The door to the room swung open and Grant Bellinger walked in and sat down across the table from one of his major contributors.

The men stared at each other in uncomfortable silence for what seemed to be forever. George spoke first:

"How could you let this happen, Grant?"

"I didn't know it was happening until about twenty minutes ago. They just told me they were arresting a bunch of Chinese mafiosos. I didn't know you were on the list. How the hell did you get involved with the likes of Hsiao Tzu?"

"It was a calculated risk. I figured that the best approach was to use a guy who was dealing with the mob. That way he is much less likely to talk, and if he talked, he was much less likely to survive to testify at trial against anyone, including me. How did the D.A.'s office get his name to begin with?"

"One of the Chinese hoods, Chan Ling, or something like that, was facing the death penalty and made a sweet deal. Gave up this guy's name. Landau jumped on it 'cause the man was supposed to have records of all his dealings. I approved the plea bargain because I figured I could take the credit for these arrests. In fact, the press conference is at 11:00 this morning, and I am scheduled to speak. Newsome said it'd be great for my campaign—and it's obvious that it's great for my campaign. But I never knew you were on the list, George. I never knew or I wouldn't have permitted it. You know that."

George believed Bellinger who had nothing to gain and everything to lose from having George arrested.

"Who interrogated Hsiao?"

"As far as I know Landau did it himself. A bit unusual, but I didn't see anything wrong with it considering that he was the one that put the plea bargain together and knew best what to ask."

"Did he confess?" George asked.

"Yes."

"Was it tape recorded?"

"I assume so. That's the procedure, although I haven't listened to the tape. I'm sure it's in the evidence room."

George stood up and began pacing around the room.

"Are we safe in here, Grant?"

"Yeah, there's no bugs in here if that's what you mean, and the detectives are busy with the others. I told them to go in alphabetical order so we'd have more time."

"Grant, remember the fund-raiser at my house?"

"How could I forget it. It raised $200,000 for my campaign, and that's just what was reported."

"Hsiao Tzu was at the fund-raiser."

Bellinger felt his head get heavy. So heavy he had to support it with his hands.

"My God, George, why? Why would you invite someone like that to my fund-raiser?"

"I never thought we would end up here. Besides, it made sense. The more contributions you got, the better were our chances, I mean, your chances of getting reelected. Landau was catching up in the polls, if you remember, and I wasn't going to take any chances. I invited everyone I knew, and at $1,000.00 a plate, I didn't think you'd complain."

"I can't believe this is happening. Two weeks before the election."

"You better get ahold of that confession tape, Grant. For your sake, you better make sure that Landau hasn't made the connection yet."

"No way. He is a young punk. If he got wind of something that juicy, he'd have it on the front page of every newspaper. There's no way he knows."

"Just the same, you better get your hands on it and make it disappear."

"George, I can't do that. Do you have any idea what would happen if I got caught?"

"You mean the same thing that's happening to me now?"

"Hey, I'm sorry about this, and I'll do what I can to get you out. I'll tell Landau there isn't enough evidence to proceed with any charges. I'll . . ."

"And you think Landau is going to be satisfied with that? Especially when you're on television every goddamn night telling the world how hard you are on criminals. He'll shove it in your face. Besides, if he's made a connection between you and Hsiao and me, you're dead."

"It makes no sense, George. If he's made the connection, why hasn't he confronted me with it or leaked it out to the press?"

"I don't know, and I'm not going to wait to find out. My freedom is at stake here, my life. And if we don't stop it now, who's to say that the Feds aren't going to get involved next under RICO or some other fucking shit like that. And then what? They'll put me in the melting pot with these gangsters and put me away for the rest of my life? Listen, Grant, and listen good." George was leaning his torso across the desk to get as close to Bellinger as the desk would allow.

"I am not doing time. I am not losing my freedom. I am going to walk out of here. Do you understand? We go back a long ways, but I am not gonna let you get back to your normal life and worry about getting reelected while I am eating prison food and sharing a cell with a guy named Bubba. Now, you either help me and yourself in the process or I'm gonna do a lot more damage to your career than Hsiao Tzu ever could. I'll make myself a sweet deal and walk out of here anyway. Do we understand each other?"

Bellinger understood clearly and he knew that George meant it. He knew that all Stone had to do was ask to speak with Landau and this would be over. Hsiao Tzu was one thing. There was room for wiggle with him as he was once removed. But George was a direct connection with proof to back it up. There would be no way out.

He just never anticipated in his twenty-three years as a lawyer and fifteen of those as a prosecutor that he would be considering committing a crime. Taking bribes never bothered him. He rationalized it as a way of getting campaign contributions and guaranteeing that the people had the best D.A. money could buy. This was different. If he did what George was demanding, he risked getting caught. On the other hand, if he did not do it and George gave him up, he would be tried and convicted for bribery and violation of election laws. Neither choice appealed to Bellinger, but only one choice gave him a chance at reelection and to keep his life as he knew it.

Why couldn't Landau have waited one more term to run for the D.A.? Bellinger only wanted one more term and then he would run for attorney general, or, better yet, governor. But no, the twerp had to run for election now, an election which, if Bellinger lost, would most likely mean the end of his career, and which, if he won, would be a perfect stepping stone to higher office.

He's worked too hard and has come too close to the next great chapter in his life to see it dissipate over some moral issue. He could do a lot more good on the moral front if he won, compensating more than sufficiently for any ethically questionable actions he may choose to undertake. Life, like law, Bellinger believed, was nothing more than an attempt to achieve balance. In law, some individual freedoms had to be sacrificed for the overall safety of the general population. Some criminals had to go free in order to protect the civil liberties of others. In life, there was the yin and the yang, the give and the take. Bellinger would take now so that he could give later.

"What do you have in mind, George?" He asked.

"First of all, get your hands on that tape and make it disappear. It could get accidentally lost or erased, couldn't it?"

"I suppose. But Landau would just get Hsiao to talk again. Besides, he is expected to testify in person at these trials."

"He won't make it." George said.

"He is under twenty-four-hour guard in an undisclosed location with two uniforms. They won't find him."

"They will if you let the location leak."

Now Bellinger was horrified. Destroying evidence was one thing, but murder . . .

"I can't be a part of this, George. I spent my whole life putting murderers behind bars. I am not going to become one just to win reelection."

"Let me explain something to you, Grant. Hsiao is going to die anyway. You don't squeal on the mob wherever they're from and live. He's an idiot. He would have been better off doing the time for money laundering. It's either Hsiao or us. It's come down to that. I see it clearly. I'm surprised you don't."

"I don't understand why he has to be killed. All we care about is getting you off and making sure that nothing gets discovered about our connection. I think we can do that."

"You think! And what if you can't. What if by the time I come up for trial you are no longer the D.A.? What then?" George was getting impatient. He didn't know how much time they had left before someone came into the interrogation room, and he had to convince Bellinger now. "How many people know about your connection with me and Hsiao?"

"Besides us?"

"Yes, besides us." George was irritated.

"Well, Hsiao, of course, but that's only if he remembers being at my fundraiser."

"Trust me. He remembers. No criminal forgets being at a fundraiser for the district attorney. Who else?"

"Well, Landau, if Hsiao confessed it to him. Chan Ling, possibly, and I would assume Chan Ling's attorney, Jackson Boyd, who made the deal with Landau."

"Precisely. Chan Ling won't testify. He's made his deal and he's not about to reappear. Besides, if anyone finds out he gave up Hsiao and that's how all these people got arrested, he won't live long in prison. Landau has nothing if he doesn't have the tape or the witness. No one will believe him. And, if we eliminate Hsiao—we're both home free."

"What about Boyd?"

"Don't worry about Boyd. I know how to take care of that. Now, where is The Little Pig?"

The Station

Tess was on her way to the downtown police station. It was 9:30 AM and the media was still camping out by the entrance. Most reporters had been there since the crack of dawn when the information about the arrests was first leaked to the press. No one knew exactly who called the press that early, but no one really cared.

Bellinger knew and he cared. Newsome made the call and prepared him for the press conference. "You can't buy this kind of publicity," he told his boss. It was perfect. At 11:00 AM Bellinger would deliver his speech, gallantly answer questions, and be a hero. They fully expected that this would carry them through to the election day.

Tess made her way through the crowd of reporters and into the police station. To her surprise, she found it louder and more chaotic than the scene outside. She approached a female officer whose name tag said "Sandy Zakowski," and explained that she may have some information for them about a Walter Manning, one of the men they arrested that morning.

She explained how she saw him on TV and that he may be involved in a fraudulent scheme with a man by the name of Charlie Parks. The officer told her to wait in the waiting area until Detective Tatum was free and he may be able to assist her, and went back to typing her report. Everyone at the station was occupied. There was no one else to approach.

Tess was not sitting down for more than five minutes when she observed the door to one of the rooms open and the man whom she recognized from the TV ads as Grant Bellinger, the district attorney, walk out and disappear down the hall. About ten minutes later, she observed a middle-aged man in plain clothes walk into the same room and almost immediately come out with another man he was loosely holding by his arm.

"That's him!" Tess exclaimed as she ran up to Officer Zakowski, who was still intent on typing. "Officer, that's the man I was telling you about. That's Mr. Manning."

Jack Tatum and his prisoner both turned to look at this excited woman pointing at George and calling him by another name. George Stone turned away and pretended not to have noticed Tess Lowe. He cursed Charlie for not being able to control his urges. George could, why couldn't Charlie? Sandy walked up to Detective Tatum and explained that the young lady had some information on his arrestee by the name of Walter Manning.

"Who? I don't remember arresting anyone named Manning." Jack brought George up to the booking clerk and gave routine instructions. He walked up to Tess and politely asked her to sit down at one of the desks.

"Detective Jack Tatum. How can I help you?" He asked Tess.

"Thank you, Detective. Thank you for talking to me. My name is Tess Lowe. That man by the counter, I've met him before. His name is Walter Manning. Supposedly, he purchased some real estate in Oregon just like I did and like many other people did. The properties were sold by a Charlie Parks who has disappeared with the money." Tess was rambling. She did not know how much time the detective would be able to devote to her, and wanted to make sure she got out all the important details.

"I saw this man on TV being arrested and it dawned on me that he was involved in this scheme from the start."

"I'm sorry, ma'am, but that man's name is George Stone. It's not Walter Manning. Now, as far as the real estate fraud you're describing, let me give you the extension for our fraud department. I'm sure they can help you." Jack opened one of the drawers and began looking for paper. His desk was at the other side of the station, and the desk he happened to be next to was in disarray.

"Stone Enterprises," Tess mumbled. "Detective Tatum, the name of the company that stole our money was Stone Enterprises. Walter Manning was obviously just an alias."

"Stone is a very common name." Jack answered thoughtfully. "Besides, I doubt that anyone who was hiding from you would use his own name on a company that served as his front. Are you sure about this being the same guy?"

"I am positive." Tess said. "Detective, please, I've lost $100,000. I know there were other people who lost hundreds of thousands of dollars. I have been trying desperately to find Charlie Parks. His apartment is vacant. He has disappeared and we have no place to turn. Please, I know I am right."

Jack walked over to George Stone who was still standing at the counter. George strained to overhear the conversation. This rationale was exactly what he counted on when he chose the name of Stone Enterprises. Who would think that a professional would use his own name. Everything was so well calculated and controlled. Everything except Hsiao Tzu, but that too was now under his control.

"That lady over there says your name is Walter Manning." Jack said to Stone. "I told her she was mistaken, but she swears you and some guy named Parks stole money from her and a bunch of other people. Now, would you happen to know anything about that, Mr. Stone?"

"No, Detective, I wouldn't. And by the way, I asked to call my lawyer over three hours ago. I am gonna get that chance, aren't I?"

"That's what I thought you'd say." Jack said more to himself than to his suspect, and returned to Tess.

"He's denying it. But I'm sure you wouldn't expect anything other than that. I'll tell you what. The stuff you're describing sure fits this guy's profile. He was arrested with the Chinese mafia, but he is a white collar guy who apparently has a serious need for money laundering."

"That's it, Detective. That's it. He's got to be the guy. It all fits. Look, I know you guys are up to your necks in alligators, but we've tried to do this on our own, without getting the police involved. For this very reason." Tess pointed around the station. "And I am happy to wait until this calms down. Frankly, we have reached the end of the line in any event. Please, whatever you can do whenever you can do it. There are a lot of hurt souls who would be enormously grateful." Tess was including herself in the count.

"Alright. Why don't you give me your name and number. This guy isn't going anywhere." Jack said. "Once the investigation gets under way, if we find any link between George Stone, Stone Enterprises, and this guy Parks, we'll get in touch with you immediately. I'm sorry. Things are kind of crazy around here. Where's the goddamn paper?" Jack snapped, opening the drawers of a stranger's desk. The officers were still busy processing the criminals and paid no attention to the frustrated detective.

"Detective, here, let me give you my business card." Tess reached over into her purse and grabbed a gold business card holder that Tommy had given her for her birthday two years ago.

"Damn it, I forgot to refill the cards," she cursed as she opened the card holder. "Look, take this, take my card holder. It has my name imprinted on it and I'm in the book. I'll just get it back from you next time."

Jack took the card holder, put it in the left pocket of his shirt and said, "We'll do everything we can to nail this guy for you." Tess was convinced of the sincerity of the intentions, but not the truth of the statement.

As Jack Tatum disappeared down the hall, Tess remained at the station with her eyes glued on George Stone aka Walter Manning. She watched the booking clerk fingerprint him, hand him a quarter, and point him to the public phone located at the other side of the room.

Stone walked over to the phone. He was, of course, entitled to his one phone call. But he made three. He used the quarter for the first call. That way they couldn't trace it to him. When he was done with that call, he dialed 411 and got the number for the Law Offices of Jackson Boyd. Using his calling card number, which he had memorized, he called Boyd's office.

At 11:00 AM precisely, Grant Bellinger held a press conference. He was poised, polished, and well informed. He took credit for obtaining evidence from a very important witness whose name and whereabouts he would not release because that man's life would be in grave danger. He took credit for the early morning arrests of dangerous criminals who have plagued this town for far too long. He proudly advised the press that one of the men arrested fit the composite of one of the bank robbers from that series of bank robberies he was sure everyone would remember. And, as if he were receiving an Oscar, at the conclusion of his prepared statement thanked the men and women of the Los Angeles Police Department and Assistant D.A. Mitchell Landau for their assistance in making this crucial contribution to the safety of the people of this town. The polls taken twenty-four hours after the press conference showed Bellinger back in the lead.

CHAPTER 7

New Orleans

Charlie arrived in New Orleans as scheduled. He took a cab to the Louisiana Inn Motel and checked in under the name of Sean Masters. This was quite a change from his accommodations in Cancun. This was a two-story, twenty-room dive. Instead of a view of the Caribbean, Charlie's room faced the parking lot. He opened his suitcase and began to unpack. He had no idea how long he would stay in this place, but it would be at least until Sunday when he would meet with George and get briefed on his new job.

New Orleans was his old stomping ground, or that of Keith Williams anyway. It had been six years since he washed dishes at Stella's Cajun Restaurant, and the statute of limitations had now run out. The Feds would be off his back, but he was still a little uncomfortable about being back here. He tried to tell George, but he would not listen.

Keith Williams was the only time Charlie had ventured on his own, and the one time he got closer to being caught than ever. The scheme he created was relatively simple and, he thought, untraceable. He opened an art stand on Bourbon Street, where he stood during the day with many others pandering to tourists anxious to purchase a memento of their trip, as if proof was necessary that they were really here. Paintings of steam boats on the Mississippi River were his biggest sellers.

Instead of taking cash, Charlie proudly displayed a Visa and MasterCard sign and took imprints of cards from unsuspecting tourists. And, so that his customers did not have to carry the paintings with them as they continued to browse and enjoy Bourbon Street and its surrounding areas, Charlie offered to deliver the souvenirs to their hotel rooms.

At that point, he knew the name, credit card number and the hotel room. While the tourists continued shopping, having lunch, and listening to jazz music, Charlie would call the hotel concierge on his cell phone, pretend he was the hotel guest, and order deliveries of a variety of items on the credit cards to another location. Gifts, mostly, he explained. Meanwhile, Charlie's assistant would take off to the hotel, and, armed with the name, the purchased painting, and the receipt, would bribe the maid to let him into the hotel room.

"I promised I would be here before they left, and I am late," Charlie's assistant would explain. "Please. I'm going to get fired if I don't get this thing into the room now."

On the back end, Charlie would then sell the credit card imprints to people who knew how to use that information much more effectively than he did. In the evenings, Charlie worked at Stella's where he really did wash dishes and get free meals. Stella Williams, a large black woman, took a liking to Charlie, or Keith, as she knew him. One day, Stella told him that an FBI agent had come in looking for him. Apparently, the people he sold the credit card numbers to were part of a major interstate ring. That was the last time, Charlie decided, that he would be the leader of the band. Too many headaches and too many risks.

It was hot and muggy outside. Charlie changed into a pair of shorts and a T-shirt, picked up his wallet and cigarettes, and left the motel. Elm Street was a couple miles away, and he could use the exercise. Mexico made him feel lazy, and he had not had his morning jog since he left L.A.

The post office on Elm Street was empty. It was the middle of a weekday afternoon. Charlie approached the only clerk behind the counter who was busy processing a package. When the clerk was finished with his task, he looked up at Charlie:

"Yes, suh."

"I need to rent a P.O. box for thirty days. Do you have any available?"

"We do. I need an I.D. and thirty dollars. The charge is ten dollars for rent, ten dollars for a key deposit, and ten dollars non-refundable processing charge."

Charlie took out his new driver's license and thirty dollars in cash. The clerk took the I.D. and the money and handed Charlie a blank form. As Charlie filled out the information on the form with his new identity, the clerk walked into the back office. He returned with Charlie's I.D., checked the form, and handed him the key.

"You have box number 357. It's on the left side. This is the key. You have to return it when you stop renting your box."

Charlie thanked the clerk and went over to the box to test out the key. It worked.

Seaside Inn

That night at the Seaside Inn in Santa Barbara, California, Hsiao Tzu was pacing in front of the only window.

"For the last time, will you sit down?" Screamed Sergeant Eddie Mozhinsky as he stuck an entire slice of pizza in his mouth. "You want your ugly head blown off?"

Hsiao Tzu sat down but continued to nervously twitch his extremities—first his hands and then his feet. He had changed his mind about testifying. In fact, he changed his mind as soon as he confessed, but it was too late. Why did he act so quickly? Why didn't he think this through? What if Chan Ling never said anything and it was all a trick? Besides, he told that man everything. Landau, wasn't that his name? They have the tape—why do they still need him? And why wasn't he given any special treatment when he insisted he knew the district attorney and was even invited to his fund-raiser. Probably because that Landau man didn't believe him.

"You want some more of this?" Mozhinsky asked his partner hoping the answer would be no.

"Nah, I've had enough of this junk food. I wish they'd relieve us, man, I actually miss my wife's cooking. Been stuck in this hell hole with this chink for three days now. Almost wish they'd blow the son of a bitch away and we could go home." Stanley Wolfson said as he was cheating at solitaire.

Suddenly, there was a knock on the door. Mozhinsky and Wolfson both took out their guns and motioned to Hsiao to get down on the floor. They'd been partners for four years and knew instinctively what the other one would do. With their guns drawn they quietly approached the door and stood on opposite sides.

There was another knock. Mozhinsky nodded his head signaling to Wolfson that he was ready.

"Yeah." Wolfson said.

"It's Tatum. Open up."

Mozhinsky and Wolfson relaxed their guns and Wolfson opened the door for the detective in charge. The Little Pig got up off the floor and sat down as soon as he felt he could bend his knees. He urinated in his pants and needed to use the bathroom, but he was too frozen with fear at the moment to move.

"What's up, Jack? We weren't expecting relief 'till tomorrow morning and certainly not you."

"The uniforms are busy with the other arrests. The guys who were arrested all got their lawyers immediately and there was no one for me to interrogate." Just as well, thought Jack, fewer interrogations, fewer times he'd have to testify in court and be cross-examined by slimy defense attorneys who were paid more for spouting nonsense for a day than he was for protecting lives for a whole year. "How's the pig?"

"He's all right," Mozhinsky said with his mouth full as he went back to the pizza. "Been shakin' since we got here."

"Either one of you guys need a break?" Jack asked taking off his coat.

"Actually, I could use a walk. There's got to be a takeout place nearby that has food that beats this shit Eddie's been swallowing like there's no tomorrow," said Wolfson.

"Go ahead. But don't be long. I only drove here to check up on you guys. I do want to get home sometime tonight."

Wolfson left. Jack Tatum walked towards the bathroom and passed Hsiao Tzu sitting on his chair and still shaking. Hsiao would have to wait again before he could take care of his soaked pants. Eddie Mozhinsky sat in his chair and pulled out Rolaids from his shirt pocket. It was a miracle drug. He could eat anything he wanted and as much as he wanted. Fifteen minutes and this stomach pain would be all gone. The knock on the door came at the same time as the flushing of the toilet. Eddie heard it. Jack didn't.

"He did it again, man, he always forgets his fucking wallet." Eddie got up slowly and walked to the door still chewing on the Rolaids tablet. Jack walked out of the bathroom drying his hands with the hotel towel. He saw Eddie unlock the door latch and reach for the door knob.

"No!" Jack screamed throwing down the towel and reaching for his gun. It was too late. A muscular Asian man kicked the door open the rest of the way and busted into the motel room with a machine gun. Another Asian man carrying a 9 mm shoved in after him. Eddie had no chance to reach for his gun as the fire from the machine gun at close range ripped apart his insides. He did not feel the shots fired into his head. He was dead before he hit the floor.

Jack, partially blocked by the wall, grabbed his gun and fired at the man with the machine gun, hitting him once in the shoulder and another, he was sure, hit his chest. The man stopped firing and fell on top of Eddie. Jack turned his gun to the second man and heard a shot, but it rang out a fraction of a second before he knew that his finger squeezed the trigger. He felt a fire burning in his left side

113

and then felt another one flare up in his stomach. He heard his own gun fire before he fell down, and then heard two more shots. The room went dark.

On the way back from a takeout place, Stanley Wolfson noticed two Santa Barbara Police Department vehicles and an ambulance in front of the Seaside Inn. He ran upstairs and towards the room. On the way, he noticed a trail of blood on the ugly hotel carpeting. The door was open. Four police officers were walking around the hotel room, and two paramedics were checking on the bodies. Wolfson stood motionless in the doorway. Just a couple of feet in front of him lay Eddie, his partner, with his eyes still open, peacefully staring at the ceiling. Slumped on top of him was a stranger who was still clinging to his machine gun. The two bodies lay in a pool of blood. The blood of a cop killed in the line of duty mixed with the blood of a murderer killed by another cop.

Hsiao Tzu was lying on the floor by the window face down with two bullet holes—both in the back of his head. He was not killed. He was executed. And to the left, in the hallway, the paramedics were hovering over Jack Tatum.

"Officer, can you answer some questions for us? Officer?"

Wolfson heard the words but didn't understand them. He dropped the containers of the Chinese food he was holding, ran into the bathroom and vomited.

The same night, the evidence room at the downtown police station was minus one cassette tape.

Later that Night

Mitch and Kari Landau were awakened at 1:30 AM by the phone. Mitch rolled over his sleeping wife and picked up the receiver:

"Yeah," he answered, rubbing the sleep out of his eyes.

"Mitch, it's Grant. We have a problem. Can you be in my office within the hour?"

"What kind of problem?"

"I'll tell you when you get here." The phone went dead.

"What's going on, honey?" Kari said wrapping herself around her husband.

"I don't know. The Dinosaur wants me in his office right away. Says we have a problem. I have to go." Mitchell dressed in the dark and left.

When he got to Bellinger's office, he found Grant sitting behind his desk. In the corner of the office sat Detective Duane Lundy.

"Come in and close the door," Bellinger ordered. "You remember Detective Lundy from the special mafia task force." Landau and Lundy nodded at each other. They had worked together on the Berardo case and, despite the conviction, there was no love lost between the two. It was nothing personal. Lundy hated all lawyers.

"What's going on?" Mitch asked sitting down.

"Hsiao Tzu is dead."

"What?" Mitchell yelled.

"Detective Lundy here has been put in charge of this investigation and has been filling me in on the details."

Bellinger nodded at Lundy giving him the floor.

"Hsiao was killed a few hours ago along with Sergeant Mozhinsky," Lundy began. "Jack Tatum apparently went there last night to check up on them and took a couple bullets. He's in the intensive care at a hospital in Santa Barbara in critical condition. They did surgery on him. Took out the bullet from his stomach. The other one is lodged near his heart and they're leaving it. It was too dangerous to remove."

"How the hell did they find out where Hsiao was?"

"Well, that's kind of what Detective Lundy and I wanted to talk to you about, Mitch."

"What is that supposed to mean?" Mitch asked.

"Well, we've been talking about it ever since we've learned of this horrible thing. There were only six people who knew where Hsiao was. Two of them are dead and one in critical condition. So I doubt they were the ones who leaked the location." Bellinger was the master of the obvious. "There was another cop named Wolfson, but he says that being relieved by Tatum was a surprise to him and Mozhinsky. So he couldn't have been the one. That leaves me and you. I know I didn't do it. I sure as hell wouldn't have done it. That leaves you."

"You're crazier than I thought, Grant. I'm the one who put the plea bargain together for Chan Ling to get Hsiao's name. I'm the one who interrogated Hsiao to get the names of the Chinese mafia. Why the hell would I want him killed?" Mitch was screaming now.

"Because you wanted me to look bad. I'm the one who held the press conference and announced these arrests. I'm still the D.A. I'm the one who will get kicked by the press because our star witness is dead. No wonder you were so eager to let me take the credit for the plea bargain and for the arrests. You tried to set me up, Landau, but it didn't work. The worst part about it is that you let a good cop go down because of your selfish political ambition. You are scum, Landau."

Bellinger looked over at Detective Lundy who had been sitting quietly watching the two gladiators go at it. He stood up, took the handcuffs off his belt and walked up to Landau.

"I'm sorry, Mr. Landau, but you're under arrest for conspiracy to commit murder."

"You son of a bitch. You're not going to get away with this. I know about you and Hsiao and your fund-raiser, and I have proof."

"It's too late, Landau. You're just trying to pin what you did on me, and it's not going to work."

As he watched his rival being taken in handcuffs out of his office, Bellinger sat back comfortably in his chair and thought about how it all worked out after all. Hsiao was dead and George would go free. As soon as the press conference is held this afternoon, Landau will be history, and he, Bellinger, was guaranteed to win reelection. He was sorry about Mozhinsky. He met him a couple of times and he seemed like a nice guy. He was very sorry about Jack. He liked Jack and hoped that he would pull through. Bellinger reached for the phone and dialed the number for Timothy Newsome. He wanted an early meeting with his campaign manager. They had a lot of preparation to do for the press conference. It had to be handled just right.

The news of Hsiao's death spread like wildfire through the holding cells. It was 5:00 AM, and George had just fallen asleep. The upper cot in his cell was a far cry from his king size bed. The cell was musty and cold. Worst of all, it smelled.

He was awakened by a loud chatter in a foreign language. When he opened his eyes, he saw his three cell mates sitting on the bottom cot across from him speaking Chinese. He knew he was a stranger to them and he knew how dangerous these men were, but for some reason he was comforted by their presence in his cell. In fact, he felt a certain camaraderie with these gangsters.

"Excuse me," George interrupted the Cantonese chatter. The three men looked up at him. George thought he saw them smiling. "Excuse me, did something happen?" The biggest man of the three prisoners stared straight at George, stood up and walked over to him. He leaned on George's cot and smiled. George was sure it was a friendly smile, but the man was missing two front teeth and looked sinister. George moved backwards until his back touched the wall.

"He gone. We free." The man said spitting as he talked.

"What he's trying to say," another man stood up and spoke in perfect English, "is that the rat who turned us all in is dead. Without the witness, they've got nothing and are going to have to let us go."

It worked, George thought with great relief. My phone call worked. He wanted to share his thrill with his cell mates. After all, he was the one who was responsible for setting them free. But this was not the time nor the place.

"It gets better," the man continued. "It was the assistant D.A. who leaked where the rat was, and he's gonna be in jail for murder while we are gonna be released. I love this country."

Son of a bitch, George thought with a contented smile. There *is* such a thing as a perfect crime. George crossed his arms, lay back on his cot, and closed his eyes. It was only a matter of time now before he was a free man. A dip in his Jacuzzi would sure feel good right now.

Jackson Boyd learned the news about Hsiao and Sergeant Mozhinsky after being awakened by the clock radio, which went off religiously at 6:00 AM. The radio also announced that Detective Tatum's condition had been upgraded from critical to serious. Jackson immediately dialed his answering service.

"At 3:00 AM you had a phone call from a Mitchell Landau, L-a-n . . ." began the operator.

"I know how to spell it. What did he say?" Jackson was irritated.

"He said it was an emergency and for you to come down to the downtown police station immediately."

"Why the hell didn't you call me with this message? Jesus, I told you people a hundred times to call me with emergency messages."

"I'm sorry, sir, but I'm new here."

"You're new. They have a new person every fucking day. Were there any other emergency calls I didn't hear about?"

"Not that I can see, Sir. Can you hold on for a minute, please? I need to answer another line." Before Jackson could respond, the phone went dead.

"Hello. Hello. Well, shit," Jackson cursed at the stranger on the other end of the receiver. "The idiot disconnected me."

When Jackson Boyd arrived at the downtown station, the camera crews were already swarming outside. He drove around the block and parked in the rear. He walked in through the back door and walked up to the booking clerk.

"Good morning, Gloria."

"What's good about it," she retorted. "I spent two days processing these pigs, and they're gonna go free. I don't know why we bother arresting and processing these assholes. They always manage to get back on the street and do it again. So, don't be expecting me to be friendly to you this morning. You're just as bad as they are, or worse even."

"I'm just doing my job, Gloria. Even the worst of criminals are entitled to the best defense under our Constitution."

"Well, maybe it's time to change the Constitution."

"Fine, call your senator. Meanwhile, can you tell me where I can find Landau. I got an emergency call from him in the middle of the night asking me to meet him here."

"That figures. He leaks where this guy is, frees these gangsters, and then calls their lawyer for help. Very clever. You lawyers are all the same."

"What are you babbling about? Who leaked what to whom? Where's Mitch?"

"He's in a holding cell. Been there since early this morning." Gloria reported.

"Well, let him know that I'm here, and bring him out, please. I must speak with him."

"Until he's properly booked, he's only allowed to see his lawyer." Gloria was obviously enjoying this.

"I am his lawyer or do you need my card?"

"Okay, you can go on in. He's down the hall and to your right. Give me a minute and I'll tell the officer to let you in."

Gloria disappeared and Jackson walked over to the vending machine. He put in two quarters, punched H-3 for black coffee, and watched it pour into a paper cup. This made no sense. Mitch wouldn't leak Hsiao's location. He didn't even want to let Chan

Ling off the hook. Why would he plea bargain Chan Ling, get Hsiao's name, have ten people arrested based on Hsiao's confession, and then have Hsiao killed just to let those criminals go? This is nonsense. Jackson took out the cup of coffee from the vending machine and began to drink it.

Suddenly, a phone conversation from yesterday popped into Jackson's mind. He was in his office when his secretary told him that there was a potential new client on the phone. Jackson took the call:

"This is Jackson Boyd," he had answered.

"Mr. Boyd. My name is George Stone," said the voice on the other end of the line. "I have been arrested and I need a lawyer. I am calling you from the police station."

"What are you arrested for, Mr. Stone?"

"Well, I'm not sure it's safe for me to speak here."

"The phones aren't bugged. Look around you and tell me if anyone is paying attention to you."

"I guess not. All right. There is one more thing. What I am going to tell you, it is privileged, isn't it?" George already knew the answer to this question.

"Yes, Mr. Stone. Since you have called me looking to retain my services as an attorney, anything you tell me is protected by the attorney-client privilege, whether you end up hiring me or not. Now, tell me, what are the charges against you?"

"Right now, it's tax evasion." George was whispering and Jackson was straining to hear. "You see, this Chinese business man, Hsiao Tzu, laundered my money. I've been running illegal business schemes for fifteen years and had never been caught."

"You got lucky."

"Luck has little to do with it. Why don't we stop playing games, Mr. Boyd. I know you represented Chan Ling. I know you and Assistant D.A. Landau made a deal and your client gave up Hsiao's name. That's how the cops got to all the other Chinese mafia people who have been arrested and that's how they got to me. They probably would have gotten to me earlier, but the D.A. and I are chummy. I've given big contributions to Grant Bellinger over the years and so has Hsiao Tzu."

"Why are you telling me all this?"

"Well, you see, Counselor, it's quite simple. Bellinger and I weren't sure if between Chan Ling and Hsiao Tzu, you and Landau had this information already. This way, whether you did or didn't, you can't tell anyone about it. Attorney-client privilege, remember? You and I both know, you open your mouth and you'll lose your license. You got any other skills, Mr. Boyd?" The phone went dead.

Jackson had been bothered by that conversation. In fact, he was pissed off about being set up that way. But what did the man really reveal to him? That he and Hsiao Tzu gave money to Bellinger's campaign. Big deal. He was sure that many criminals contributed to campaigns of the politicians who were least likely to get interested in them. Certainly, if he were a criminal, he would choose Bellinger over Landau any day. But this conversation with Stone was taking on a different meaning now. Something wasn't right. The same night that this man called him, Hsiao got killed and Mitchell got arrested. Jackson stared at the bottom of the empty coffee cup, threw the cup out, and proceeded to meet with his newest client.

In a grey cold holding cell, Mitchell Landau was pacing. In the last few hours, he ran the scenario through his head at least a hundred times. He was sure he knew exactly what happened, and he would have this all solved as soon as Boyd helped him get that tape out of the evidence room.

"Mitch," Jackson walked into the room.

"Jackson, thank you for coming." Mitch was relieved to see the man who was his adversary so many times in the courtroom.

"I would have been here sooner, but my stupid answering service didn't give me your message until this morning, and only after I called them."

"I assume you heard about Hsiao Tzu."

"Yeah. It was the first thing I heard on the radio this morning when I woke up. The camera crews are already outside the station."

"Anything about my arrest?"

"Not yet. Bellinger must be saving it for the press conference this afternoon."

"Good. That gives us time. I haven't even told Kari. She thinks I've been working all night. The son of a bitch called me in this morning saying we had a problem. I walk into his office and he has me arrested. Jackson, I know what happened and I need your help. I know who killed Hsiao Tzu, or at least, who leaked his location so that he would be killed, and I know enough about Bellinger to end his career."

"Look, Mitch, despite our roles in the courtroom, I consider you a friend, but I have no desire to get in the middle of your battle with Bellinger. Now, if you want to hire me to represent you, that's another matter."

"Jackson, yes, of course I want you to represent me. You're the best defense attorney I have ever gone against."

"Tell me what you know." Boyd said.

"All right," Mitchell started as he sat down. "After we made the deal with Chan Ling, I interrogated Hsiao myself. I wanted everything the guy knew, including whatever he knew about Bellinger. Specifically, I wanted to know what Hsiao was doing at his fund-raiser. I have to admit I was driven by more than my job as the assistant D.A. I wanted to bury Bellinger. As I suspected, Hsiao was full of information. I was surprised that he talked. But after I mentioned Chan Ling to him and that the guy was doing only five years for murder, I think he saw his opportunity to get off the hook. Obviously, he didn't think he would get killed.

"Anyway, after Hsiao tells me about his records, and offers to decode them if we give him a deal, I asked Hsiao about the fund-raiser. The guy's eyes lit up. I guess he thought Bellinger would be his ticket out of there and that I was giving him that opportunity. He told me that a client of his, George Stone, called him and invited him to his house for a thousand-dollars-a-plate dinner for the D.A. Hsiao was more than happy to pay, figuring that this is his 'get out of jail free' ticket. Not an unfounded thought, as it turns out. He told me Stone had been chummy with the D.A. for many years and wanted to make sure Bellinger got reelected, so he was holding this bash at his house. Said he saw Stone and Bellinger acting like they were joined at the hip, like they knew each other for years and were best of friends."

Jackson listened intently. He realized now that the phone call to his office was no fluke. It was all part of a well organized plan intended to put him right in the middle of it.

"I got it all on tape, Jackson. It's all there."

"If you had it on tape, why didn't you go public with it then?"

"I wanted to. Believe me, I ached to go to the press, anonymously or otherwise. But I thought it through then. All Bellinger had to do to get out of it was pretend he didn't know anything about George Stone's criminal activities. And Hsiao, well, there were probably two hundred people at that fund-raiser according to Hsiao. Bellinger would have said he couldn't have known everyone who was there. No. I had to wait until Stone was arrested and Bellinger knew about it. I had to wait until Bellinger got up in front of the cameras at a press conference and bragged about the convictions. Then, there was no way out.

"I would have taken that tape to the press, and Bellinger would be gone. That was my plan anyway, but something went wrong. I think Stone and Bellinger spoke and planned to have Hsiao killed and me arrested. Bellinger and I were the only people who could have leaked the location where Hsiao was being kept. I obviously didn't do it. So, I figure Bellinger told Stone, and Stone made a phone call and had Hsiao killed. A perfect plan, except for one thing. The tape. They don't know what's on the tape. See, they figure that it's just Hsiao's confession which is nothing without the live witness. They don't know I've got Bellinger nailed on that tape."

"You're right. With that tape, in one swoop you'll exonerate your-self and put the suspicion on Bellinger. But how are you going to get that tape out of the evidence room?"

"That's where you come in. Jackson, I need that tape. You have to get it for me. If you're my lawyer, you can get access to it and duplicate it."

"All right. You've got yourself a lawyer for now. I'm going to need a retainer, Mitch. Sorry, but business is business. Let's say $25,000 to start, another $25,000 if you get indicted, and another $25,000 if I've got to try this thing."

"That's a lot of money, Jackson, but I'm not going to get indicted. In fact, I'm not sure that I will be arraigned. They have no evidence against me, and you're going to help me get evidence that will ruin Bellinger. Once you get it, I'll be out of here, and Bellinger will be in here. You can then represent him and make your money." Mitch was only half joking with the last comment.

None of his clients ever believed there was any evidence against them, Jackson pondered. All of his clients always thought they wouldn't get indicted or tried. It was interesting that the pattern held even for the assistant D.A.

"Look, if you're right about Bellinger, the moment he gets wind that I'm your lawyer and I've made a request for that tape, the tape will disappear."

"That's why you have to go right now. And better yet, don't tell any-one you're going in after the tape for me. Go in for one of your other clients. You know this is the right thing to do, Jackson."

Jackson knew it was the right thing to do, especially when he had the evidence in his head to exonerate his new client. But even if he told Mitchell about his conversation with George Stone in violation of the Canon of Ethics, it would be inadmissible in a court of law, and Jackson would be guaranteed an early retirement from the practice of law. He wasn't ready for that. On the other hand, there was noth-ing wrong with getting the tape for one of his other clients. Da Matzu, for example. After all, the tape did have Hsiao's confession on it where he fingered Da Matzu.

"You know Da Matzu?" he asked Mitch.

"Yeah, I've seen his file. He is being charged with those bank robberies. He matched the composite. Is he one of yours?"

"He hired me yesterday. So did Bao Tsing. But I figure Bao is going to walk without Hsiao Tzu. Da is going to stay because of the composite—it's evidence independent of Hsiao's testimony. Alright, before Bellinger gets wind of this, I'm going to the evidence room and try to retrieve the tape. Meanwhile, you better call your wife. The media is likely to get wind of this sooner rather than later. You don't want her learning of this from the TV."

"I'll call her. Get the tape."

Jackson Boyd walked into the evidence room at the downtown station and walked up to the counter. The clerk recognized him.

"Hello, Counselor. You must be a busy one these days. Looking for something in particular?"

"Yeah. I'm representing Da Matzu, one of the Chinese men arrested two days ago. His arraignment is on Monday and I understand you guys are holding the confession tape."

"Well, can't say I know anything about the case, but then again, I can't say I care. How come the prosecutor isn't giving it to you?"

"Oh, with everything going on they're so busy and confused, I thought I'd come to the source."

"O.K. Fill this out and leave your driver's license with me. You know you can't leave here with it and I've got to follow you where you're going."

"I know the procedure." Jackson filled out the form with the name of Da Matzu as his client, and Hsiao Tzu as the person giving the confession. He then took out his driver's license and left it on the counter.

"Follow me," said the clerk as he led Jackson to that location on the metal shelves where he would expect the tape to be alphabetically.

When they approached the shelf designated with the letter "H," the clerk stared at the card and then at the shelf.

"That's funny," he said scratching his head.

"What's wrong?"

"Should have been right here. Someone must have it out. The D.A. maybe."

"Are you sure? Are you sure it's not under 'T' for 'Tzu.' Certainly someone could have thought that was his last name." Jackson could not believe that the tape was missing. He knew Landau would not believe it either.

"I'm positive. It was supposed to be here. I can check for you under 'T' but I'm sure it was supposed to be here. Let me check the log and see if anyone checked it out."

Jackson and the clerk walked over to the evidence kept under the letter 'T' but found no confession tape. Likewise, the log showed nothing.

"I'm sorry, Counselor," the clerk apologized with sincerity. "I just don't know what could have happened to it. I'm gonna have to check with Phil who worked the night shift. Maybe he knows."

"You do that," Jackson said as he stormed out of the room. The one piece of evidence that could have absolved Mitchell Landau, nailed Bellinger, and relieved Jackson of his burden of having information he could never release, was gone.

CHAPTER 8

The Bullet

For the last three days, Kate Tatum sat at her husband's side in the intensive care unit in the St. Joseph's hospital in Santa Barbara. The last words she said to Jack before he left that day for work were her usual, "Try not to get killed." Despite the many years of marriage, the tender relationship they shared, the fact that she knew that her husband never doubted her devotion, and that this phrase that became part of their morning routine conveyed her love, she regretted saying it. Why couldn't she have simply said, "I love you."

She got the call when they were taking him to the hospital in an ambulance. They did not know if he would make it. She was two hours away. It was the longest two hours of her life. When they went places, especially longer distances, Jack always drove. When they would drive to their condo in Palm Desert, that drive was also two hours long, and she and Jack would talk about everything on the way, from things in their past that they had already shared with each other during their long marriage, but which somehow bore repeating, to things in their future that they looked forward to sharing. Sometimes, they just drove in silence, the comfort of which only comes with years of tending to a relationship.

This drive was hell. She kept the cell phone on the seat next to her, afraid that it would ring, and, at the same time, fearful that she would fumble reaching for it, if it did. When she got to the hospital, Jack was in surgery. All they could tell her is that one bullet was removed from his stomach, and that they were working on the other one, near his heart. They made no promises, and, as much as Kate wanted to hear good news, she appreciated the directness and honesty from the medical staff. That way, if they told her good news, she could believe them.

Four hours later, the surgeon emerged from the operating room and took off her cap.

"We were able to remove both bullets," said Dr. McCleary, "but he is still in critical condition. He lost a lot of blood, and we will have to monitor him very carefully over the next few days. But," the doctor smiled, "he's a tough bear. I've got a good feeling about this."

That was three days ago. The monitor was beeping routinely, and Kate was now used to the sound. Periodically, she would still look up and check it. Just to make sure. His breathing was steady, his chest rising and falling in tune with the monitor tones. But he was still unconscious. Kate sat at Jack's bedside and read to him. Golf magazines, mostly. In a light moment, she and Dr. McCleary concluded that the articles were much more likely to put one to sleep than to awaken him. But, it was what he wanted. What he liked.

On day four, Jack Tatum woke up. When his eyes could focus, he saw the soft and kind face of his wife.

"Oh, God. Thank God." Kate cried. "You're awake. I'm so happy that you're awake. I love you," she hurried to say.

"Where am I?" Jack asked.

"You're in Santa Barbara, in the hospital. You were shot, honey, but you'll be fine."

"I'm thirsty." Jack said.

Kate reached over for a plastic container of water with a bent straw and let her husband sip from it. Jack lifted his head, took two sips and cringed in pain. He swallowed hard and lay back on the pillow. Dr. McCleary walked into the room. She smiled and nodded at Kate.

"Well, hello there, Detective. How are we feeling?"

"We're feeling like shit, but I guess we're lucky to be alive. I am alive, aren't I?" Jack asked.

"Oh yes." The doctor answered, examining Jack's chart. "The nurse will be here in a minute to change the IV bag and get you some pain killers. They're going to make you groggy, but sleep is the best thing for you now. So, don't worry about staying awake. Now that Kate hovered over you for days to get you to wake up, you go ahead and go right back to sleep."

Jack took another sip of water from the cup.

"By the way, who is Tess Lowe?" Dr. McCleary inquired when she was done writing.

"Who?" Jack asked taking another sip of water.

"Tess Lowe. You should remember that name, Detective. She saved your life." The doctor said and left the room.

Jack looked puzzled at his wife.

"You had a business card holder in your left pocket, dear," Kate explained. "The doctor said it saved your life because it diverted the bullet. Otherwise, it would have hit your heart." Kate's voice trembled.

Jack squeezed her hand hard and closed his eyes. He tried to remember how the business card case got into his pocket and who gave it to him, but his head hurt too much to think. He fell back asleep.

The Clue

It was 2:00 AM, and she was still awake. For the last two weeks, insomnia had become part of her daily regimen, and Tess was getting used to it. Her mind would not stop working, but the rest of her system seemed to cease functioning properly. She barely ate.

Tommy had called a couple more times. He checked with some lawyers who handled these types of cases. None of them had anything encouraging to say. He would keep trying. The last time he called, he asked if he could see her. She declined. This was no time to restart something, if there was anything to restart. Nor has anything changed. They were still two people looking through different kaleidoscopes at the rest of their lives. And even if she were to set aside these differences in exchange for temporary comfort, she would always question the reasons they got back together.

She learned of the murder of the star witness for the prosecution on TV, and watched Grant Bellinger blame his assistant D.A. for the leak of the witness's location. She watched in disbelief as the media followed the release of the same men who just two days before were arrested and ceremoniously paraded like a fisherman displaying his biggest catch. And she cried helplessly as she watched one of those men, whom she knew as Walter Manning, walk out a free man while the detective she was counting on for help was reported to be in intensive care. Many nights she stayed awake in bed with the escrow papers from The Oregon Project spread out on her covers. The first couple of nights she read them thoroughly over and over again as if looking for clues.

She stopped blaming herself. Between her, Jim, and Milly, they had taken reasonable steps to check this out. Even being blinded by Charlie, she still had called the secretary of state. They had confirmed that Stone Enterprises was a Delaware corporation authorized to do business in the State of California and Oregon. Jim's lawyer, Mason West, had reviewed the agreements and the corporate documents. Tess thought of taking the documents to Tommy to review, but her pride had stopped her. The CPA's gave their seal of approval to this investment opportunity and asked if there was room for more investors as they wanted to invest personal funds.

Charlie had given Tess the same list of references that he gave to Jim and Milly. One afternoon, after Charlie left, Tess had pulled out the list and dialed the first number. After the third ring, a man had answered. She remembered the conversation:

"May I speak with Mr. Howard Barnes, please."

"This is he," answered a mature voice.

"Mr. Barnes. My name is Tess Lowe. I was given your number by Mr. Charlie Parks of Stone Enterprises. I understand that you have invested in The Oregon Project. Do you have a few minutes?"

"Yes, sure, Ms . . . ? I am sorry, what was your name again?"

"Lowe."

"Yes, Ms. Lowe. I bought four properties from Stone Enterprises about three months ago, and I've been receiving my monthly checks. You know, I am a CPA by profession, and extremely conservative, as you can imagine. I review these types of investments every day for clients, and this is the best thing I have seen come across my desk. In fact, I have decided to reinvest the money I am receiving monthly back into the project."

When Tess ran out of questions, she thanked Barnes for his time, and hung up the phone reassured. She did not know that in the back office of Century Escrow, George Stone aka Howard Barnes hung up the phone which had three separate lines. He expected the other two to ring, but they remained silent. Linda Sanders and Kevin Wilson would have answered the other two lines as Claire Meyers and Anthony Letteau respectively—the other two names on the reference list.

By 4:00 AM, Tess had finished her fourth glass of wine. She hoped that the alcohol would help her sleep. It did not. It did, however, give her a pounding headache. She got out of bed, walked into the bathroom and opened the medicine cabinet. She took two aspirin tablets out of the bottle and stared at her reflection in the cabinet mirror. Her blonde silky hair now looked like clumps of white straw. There were wrinkles on her face and bags under her eyes. She swallowed the aspirin with tap water. "This has got to stop," she thought. She walked back to her bed, sat down and, out of habit, again picked up one of the escrow papers from The Oregon Project. Suddenly, her eyes focused on the Oregon mailing address for Stone Enterprises. It was a P.O. box.

The Arraignment

The courtroom was familiar, but the feeling was strange. So many times he sat at the counsel table on the other side of the court-room, the one next to the jury box, where the prosecution side always sat—as if justice was achieved easier by that physical con-nection to that all-important place where the jury of your peers sat and passed judgment.

This time, however, Mitchell Landau was separated from the jury box—a distance of just a few feet, which seemed endless. The court-room was filled with a familiar hush of reporters starving for that juicy bit that will bring them favor with the boss and, eventually they hoped, a place on those coveted front pages that have recently been filled with screaming headlines about the assistant D.A. implicated in a murder plot that freed the mob.

In a flash, Mitch went from a gallant challenger of the old and stale political office to a man whose political ambition took him to the ultimate extreme where there were no rules and no lines. But Mitch understood that the most powerful institution in America was not any of the three branches of government or big business. It was in fact the media. An institution that, in an extraordinary way, combined the given paper power of the government with the earned money power of the biggest corporate institutions. And most importantly, unlike the government and business, the media went virtually unchecked, for the only institution powerful enough to control it and limit it was the media itself. Mitch knew this, and he also knew that the media was going to make him or break him, more than Bellinger ever could. Especially now.

Bellinger assigned his lackey, Lance Wenke to prosecute this case.

"All rise." The bailiff commanded. "The court is now in session. The Honorable Judge Betty Spencer presiding."

Spencer took the bench and looked directly at Landau.

"Good morning, Counsel."

"Good morning, Your Honor." All lawyers responded in unison.

"In the matter of *People v. Mitchell Landau*, do we have a plea?"

"Not guilty, Your Honor." Mitchell stated.

"What say you regarding bail, Mr. Wenke?"

"Thank you, Your Honor. The People recognize that Mr. Landau has no prior record and we do not consider him to be a danger to society."

"How nice of them," Mitch whispered to Jackson Boyd seated to his right and taking notes.

"However," Wenke continued, "This is a serious charge of conspiracy to commit murder and there is always a risk that the defendant, faced with these charges, will attempt to flee. Therefore, People request that bail be set at half million dollars."

Mitch gasped and sank in his seat. Jackson stood up as Judge Spencer turned her gaze to him.

"Your Honor. The prosecution is yet to come up with one shred of evidence to even hold my client, to say nothing of convicting him. I think we all know that this is a political game with intended devastating results for my client."

"Mr. Boyd. Bail?" Judge Spencer directed Jackson to the issue at hand.

"$250,000.00 Your Honor. More is simply unnecessary and unjustified."

"Bail is set at $250,000.00. Now, there's been a special request made by the defense that the preliminary hearing take place this week. Any problems with that, Mr. Wenke?"

"There is, indeed, Your Honor. We simply cannot prepare that quickly. We . . ."

"Then try harder, Mr. Wenke. You must admit this is a rather unusual situation which calls for a strict time line. The preliminary hearing is set for Thursday at 10:00 AM. If you are not ready by then, Mr. Wenke, I will dismiss the charges. Is that understood?"

"Yes, Your Honor."

Spencer stood up and unceremoniously left the courtroom. As the reporters piled out, Wenke approached Boyd.

"I think you and your client ought to seriously consider a deal while we are still in the dealing mood."

"Go to hell, Lance," Mitch snapped.

"Well, well, Jackson, doesn't look like you got much client control." Wenke remarked snootily. "Who's going to be trying this case anyway?"

"You know damn well this thing isn't going to trial. You don't even have enough evidence to get past the preliminary hearing. All you've got is Bellinger and, believe me, if there is one cross-examination I am looking forward to it's that one. Now, if you'll excuse us, we've got work to do." Jackson responded.

Mel

Mel Rittner arrived at his furniture rental store at the usual time— 6:30 AM. The store didn't open until 10:00 AM, but he was a morning person and loved to crunch numbers in his office in the wee hours of the morning. He parked in the parking lot in back and approached the entrance to the rear door of the warehouse, unlit cigar in mouth, and an old grey briefcase in hand.

"Hello, Mel." Tess was waiting for him at the door.

"You're back. I guess you're still looking for your Prince Charming." Mel retorted opening the door. Tess followed him into his office.

"I told you I couldn't help you."

Tess took out a card from her purse and put it on Mel's desk.

"What's this?" he asked.

"It's a card of Detective Jack Tatum of the LAPD."

"I can see that. What's it got to do with me?"

"Well, Mel," Tess began to speak leaning on the edge of Mel's desk. "Detective Tatum was assigned to help me search for Charlie Parks. You see, I'm not pregnant, and I am not looking for Mr. Parks for personal reasons. Mr. Parks and another man had an illegal scheme going where they stole hundreds of thousands of dollars from people. Detective Tatum was just getting started on the trail of Mr. Parks at my request when he was shot. He is now in intensive care but he is improving. When he gets better, I am going to have to tell him that he should start his investigation by talking to you. So your choice is simple, Mel. You either tell me where Mr. Parks is or you can tell Detective Tatum when he gets out of the hospital, and I can guarantee you I am much more pleasant to talk to."

Mel stared at Tatum's card and then at Tess. He hated aggressive women, especially when they were pretty. But he hated cops more.

"Why didn't you say so to begin with?" he said with a contorted smile. "I didn't know there was something criminal going on. I just thought it was a personal thing, you know." Mel reached in the drawer of his desk and pulled out a thin manila file.

"Look, I don't want any trouble with the law. I'm a law abiding citizen. Here. Here it is. He called me a couple days ago. Believe me, I wasn't too thrilled to hear from him—could've used the money. Anyway, he gave me this P.O. box in New Orleans for me to send his refund. Guess that's where he's hiding. Here's a pen, you can write this down. I don't mind." Mel handed Tess a pen and she anxiously took down the information.

"Thank you, Mel. I really do appreciate your help," Tess said heading out the door.

"By the way, lady, I don't know if this is important or not, but he told me to make the check payable to Sean Masters, some friend of his. Said he didn't have an account there yet, and this Masters guy would cash it for him."

The Jail Cell

Kari Landau was on her way to see her husband. She had finished making bail arrangements, which had cost her family $25,000, the typical 10 percent of the amount. She also had to secure payment with their home. But all that paled in comparison to her husband sitting in jail accused of conspiracy to commit murder.

When Mitch first called to tell her that Bellinger had him arrested, her first reaction was to walk into Bellinger's office and kill him. Not figuratively. Literally. And although intellectually Kari understood perfectly how illogical that overwhelming desire was, that was the thing about overwhelming desires. They made you believe that all else was unimportant and, indeed, irrelevant.

They would not need to find her after she killed Bellinger. She would proudly confess. "He was a lying asshole and a maggot," she would tell them in her confession. "He had no redeeming qualities, and I killed him because he deserved to die. Out of the gene pool."

As a prosecutor, she knew full well that this was far from a proper defense, but, as an infuriated wife, a defense was not necessary. It would be jury nullification. If you could convince a jury that a battered wife had a right to kill her husband, then, conversely, you should certainly have the right to kill to avenge your husband.

When the ire diminished, albeit slightly, she knew that Mitch needed her, more than ever, and that killing Bellinger, although a rather satisfying fantasy, was not a proper use of her energy.

"I'm here to see my husband, Mitchell Landau," she told an officer at the front desk.

"Sorry, but he is only allowed his lawyer right now." The officer answered politely.

"I am his lawyer." Kari responded reaching for her bar card in her wallet. She had not practiced law for five years, but she paid her bar dues religiously. She was on a sabbatical, as she thought of it. Sammy was three years old, and she was ready, no, anxious to get back to work. But going back to the prosecutor's office was out of the question. She quit when Bellinger insisted that Mitch and she stop seeing each other.

"She'll turn around and sue you and me both for sexual harassment." He had told Mitch.

"You have no right to tell us not to date. You know damn well that it's unconstitutional." Mitch responded.

But the die was cast. This fight with Bellinger would simply distract Mitch from his all but certain ascent to the top. She gave up her post to let him thrive. Then came Sammy.

"Alright. I'll take you to him." The officer said leading Kari down a short corridor.

Mitch was sitting on the edge of his cot. He stood upright when he saw Kari approaching. The officer unlocked the cell, and Kari walked in heading straight for her husband. They hugged hard.

"You were right." Mitch said before he let Kari go. "Bellinger is a fucking monster."

"I posted bail. It should make its way here any moment. We should be driving home in no time." Kari said.

They sat on the cot next to each other, silent for a few minutes.

"I am going to see Bellinger." Kari said.

"Why? What could possibly be accomplished with that?" Mitch asked.

"I don't know. But it feels right. I can't sit here knowing that his mug is smiling."

"He won't be smiling for long. Jackson is preparing for the preliminary hearing and I don't see any way that Spencer is going to let this thing take up any more than maybe two hours of her court time. After I'm released, we can put our heads together and get this son of a bitch."

"Mitch, you and I both know that it isn't about the preliminary hearing. And as much as you and I both want to see you as the D.A., this is beyond you now. A district attorney has falsely accused his colleague of conspiracy to commit murder just so he can win an election. And what about the tape? What about the fact that the tape is missing? He has either destroyed or ordered the destruction of evidence." Kari said.

"I think we can do this in the courtroom. The way we discussed. Jackson will cross-examine Bellinger in front of the press. He's good, Kari. He is really good. Believe me, I wish we had that goddamn tape, but it's gone. What about Stone?"

"No luck. His neighbors have not seen him, and his trail is cold." Kari reported.

"Damn, I wish Jack was well. He's got the sense of a hound. He could track that bastard." Mitch got up and walked over to the bars that separated him from the outside world ever so temporarily. But, nonetheless, this is how it felt to be on the inside. He had put many in this position.

"Mitch. Have you thought about the possibility that Spencer will find that there is sufficient evidence to hold you over for trial?" Kari asked.

"No. I don't see it. They've literally got nothing."

"But they had nothing when they arrested you, and yet, they did. And what if she does hold you over. You know how low the standard is on a preliminary hearing. What if she does and a jury is empanelled and, somehow, all the stars line up against you and you are convicted. The lack of evidence leaves this as a credibility contest. What if the jury believes that Bellinger did not do it and, by simple process of elimination, they conclude that you did. You clearly both had motive, but you are the only one on trial."

"You are talking crazy, Kari. That's impossible."

"What about Trevor Hamelynck?" Kari asked.

"That was a complete anomaly. One of those one-in-a-million cases." Mitch rebuffed.

"Mitch. You and I were both convinced he was guilty. I know we just assisted. I know we were just underlings at that time, but a jury took what amounted to no evidence and decided that he was guilty. If it weren't for the confession of a cohort nine years later, he would still be serving a twenty-year term for a crime he did not commit. Mitch, he wasn't even there. He wasn't there for the armed robbery, but he spent nine years in prison." Kari paused. Mitch remained silent, leaning against the metal bars.

Mitch remembered the case. He remembered when Trevor Hamelynck was arrested. He remembered just as vividly when he was convicted. They had no more than a composite. A night guard at an expensive equipment facility, working with the police artist, arrived at the composite. The guard was hit on the head from behind with a gun and lost consciousness. When he came to, he saw four men loading the equipment into a truck. He said he could only identify one.

They had nothing but a composite, but an overzealous cop and a driven prosecutor were determined to convict. Convict. Conviction. They were convinced and, therefore, they would convince a jury and the jury would convict. Lack of evidence was no match for the fervent desire for justice. Reasonable doubt was no barrier to judicial vengeance. Nine years later, as part of a plea bargain following another armed robbery, one of the others involved in the old crime gave up the real criminal.

"Mitch. He was innocent. You are innocent. And you are accused of conspiracy to commit murder. I know Jackson is a great lawyer. I trust him. But I have to do something. Remember that night in the car after we had dinner at The Gallery?"

Mitch remembered.

"You said to me, 'Don't ask me to be less than who I am.' I now ask you the same. I can't be and won't be less than who I am. I will not take a chance, however remote, that you are going down and I am doing a fraction less than what I can."

At that moment, a guard came over to tell them that the bail had been posted, and Mitch was free to go. That is, until the preliminary hearing.

CHAPTER

Koh Samui

Koh Samui is a small island off the Gulf of Thailand. It is about one hour flight southeast from Bangkok. "Koh" means *island* in Thai and the locals refers to the island as "Samui." Samui is a remote desolate tropical island where the poverty of the people is outweighed only by their unending smiles. Just like most of the Thai population, which is dirt poor, they have accepted their fate and seem to wallow in the warmth of their spirit.

George Stone sat on a lounge chair by the huge black bottom pool at the Santiburi Hotel on Koh Samui drinking cold Singha beer. Beer was not his alcohol of choice, but the heat and humidity made it the only beverage that could quench his thirst. He left within two days after being let out of that horrible jail cell. He knew that, despite being freed this time, his name was now on the list and they would be watching him. Who "they" were, he was not quite sure. A lot would depend on Bellinger's victory and his next term. But his relationship with Bellinger would never be the same.

Stone knew that he was the only one that could finger Bellinger in the murder of Hsiao Tzu and that made him a hot commodity. But he also figured that in the grand scheme of things, compared with the election, the arrests, Hsiao Tzu, he was small potatoes, and the extreme measures that he went to in order to cover his tracks should stop anyone looking for him, a little known white-collar criminal who hurt no one but those who were stupid enough to get hurt.

He was safe here. If they checked the airlines, they would only find his final destination as Hong Kong. From there, he changed planes to Bangkok and then to Koh Samui. He picked up a new passport in Hong Kong from his connections there and traveled in Southeast Asia under the alias of "Vincent Taylor."

The only person who knew his location was his real estate agent, a trusted friend, and even more trusted with an extra $25,000 in his bank account. The marching orders George gave were to sell the house in Bel Air quietly and quickly and to wire the money to Vincent Taylor's account in Bangkok. The rest of George's liquid assets had already been wired. The cash in bank accounts in Los Angeles, the stocks and bonds, all in all close to $1.5 million was transferred to the Siam Bank in Bangkok to the account of Vincent Taylor, the American citizen and international businessman. Siam Bank was only too happy to have such a big new client.

There was only one loose end and that was the house. George had enough money to last him in Thailand for the rest of his life. The cost of living here was cheap and he could live like a king. But that wasn't the point. He was not going to stay here forever. He planned to return to the United States in about six months to a year depending on how quickly the fuss over the district attorney election died down and what, if anything, was going to happen with the Little Pig's murder. But if Bellinger lost, he could not afford to wait to sell his house. He was keenly aware that Landau could and would seize his assets.

George spoke once with Charlie before he left. He called him at his hotel in New Orleans to tell him that their future plans were on hold temporarily. That he, George, had to leave town for a while and did not know when he would be back. Charlie had asked if he could house-sit while George was gone—a perfect solution according to Charlie. But George told him that his house was for sale. Charlie asked if he could help with the sale for a small piece, but George declined apologetically, saying that he had already given the sale to his old friend, Reggie Blair.

George felt a bit bad for Charlie, leaving him on his own, but he knew that Charlie would find his way as he did before he met George. Besides, the kid knew the risks when he got involved. Or, at least, he should have.

Law Offices of Jackson Boyd

The next morning, Mitch and Jackson were meeting in his office. They had a short window of time to prepare for the preliminary hearing.

"They have no evidence," Jackson said. "In fact, the only witness they have is Bellinger himself so he can testify as to the people who knew where Hsiao was being held and the fact that he did not disclose it. They'll never find the killers, so proving conspiracy is going to be impossible. If this morning was any indication, Spencer has already made up her mind and she'll dismiss the charges. You'll never be tried."

"I know all this, Jackson." Mitch replied. "I am looking beyond this now. I am going to prove that it was Bellinger who conspired to commit murder and then obstructed justice by having me arrested. The way I figure it, he's looking at twenty-five to life, and not a moment too short."

"And how to you plan to accomplish this without the tape?"

"There is only one person who can help us. It was George Stone who threw the fund-raiser for Bellinger that Hsiao attended. I am certain that there is a lot more to their relationship than fund-raising. Stone may have walked this time, but he'll be looking over his shoulder for the rest of his life now that we are on to him. He might want to wipe the slate clean by giving up his old pal. After all, it was Bellinger's stupidity that got him arrested to begin with. He didn't even bother looking at the search warrants before they went out. I say we get to Stone and make him a deal."

Jackson was quiet. He stood up and walked over the window of his twenty-second floor office in the Century City Towers.

"Kari said that he disappeared and has not been seen since he was released. But I don't believe he cannot be found. I think we should hire a private eye, find him and . . . Jackson. Are you listening to me?"

Jackson walked back to his desk and sat down.

"Look, Mitch," he spoke slowly and deliberately. "I'll represent you in your case. I'll get you off without a problem. But don't ask me to help you with Stone, and don't ask for my advice on that subject. And, more importantly, don't ask me why."

Mitch didn't have to ask why. There was only one reason that Jackson would say this, and, as a lawyer, Mitch knew precisely what it was.

"You know something that can help me, don't you? Stone is either a client of yours or wanted to be."

"You know I can't tell you anything. So, please don't even go there. Don't even ask."

"I'm right, aren't I?" Mitch stood up and began pacing.

"Mitch, please sit down, you are making me dizzy."

"I am your client. Screw the attorney-client privilege. This is my future we are talking about."

"And mine." Jackson replied sternly. "I honestly wish I could help you. Believe me, Mitch, I hate carrying this shit around. But I am not going to risk my license, and you know damn well that I would lose it. I'm sorry. But you have to get to Stone on your own."

"I can't believe this." Mitch said. "And you don't think that Bellinger had anything to do with this? He is playing both of us, Jackson. That motherfucker is playing both of us."

"Mitch, what do you want me to do?" Jackson asked sincerely, but knew he was posing a question where the answers were limited before they were given.

Kari took the elevator to the thirty-fifth floor. She took this ride many times before. Every morning, dressed in a business suit, carrying a briefcase. Except for those mornings when she went directly to court. Kari Landau, Esq., for the People. This time, no suit, no briefcase. She was carrying something else.

She walked out of the elevator and headed straight for Bellinger's office. His secretary did not try to stop her. Not after she saw the look on Kari's face. She swung the door open into Bellinger's private office, and closed the door behind her.

"Kari," Bellinger said reluctantly acknowledging his visitor. He stood up from his desk and nervously started to walk around. He was not unfamiliar with Kari's temper, and thought it might be best to open the door.

"Find a spot and plant yourself," Kari said calmly. "You and I are going to have a conversation."

Bellinger stopped in his tracks.

"Sit down," Kari commanded.

"Look, Kari, if what you want is to have a conversation, I think you are going about it the wrong way."

"I'm going about it the wrong way?" Kari interrupted. "You're kidding, right?"

"I don't think you want to threaten me. Isn't your family already in enough trouble?"

"I am not going to threaten you." Kari said standing straight up in perfect posture. "I am simply going to tell you exactly what is going to happen—a prediction, shall we say. No law against predicting things, if I recall correctly.

"Tomorrow morning, the day before the preliminary hearing, you are going to announce that, upon due consideration, the charges against Mitch were unfounded and they are going to be dismissed. And if you do not do that, I will see to it personally that your life, in or out of this office, is a living hell. I will spend every waking moment following your every move and taking you down either in one full swoop or one torturous step at a time."

"We are not having this conversation, Kari. You know as well as I do that it is now in the hands of the court. The train has left the station. Besides, I do not agree that there is a lack of evidence. I think that the only evidence leads to your husband. He killed a man, Kari—any way you look at it. And you are threatening a district attorney in front of a witness."

It was then, for the first time, that Kari noticed Timothy Newsome. He was sitting on the couch behind the door and to Kari's back.

"Good." Kari said unabated. "Someone who will be able to confirm that I correctly predicted the rest of your life. By the way," Kari added, "how is the search for that killer going? You know, the one that escaped from that hotel room in Santa Barbara after shooting Jack Tatum and, more probably than not, the one who put the bullets into the back of Hsiao Tzu's head? Interesting how the resources of this office seem to be focused on convicting my husband more than finding the shooter. Feeling my breath on the back of your neck yet?"

With that, Kari walked out of the office.

Surprise!

Leaning on his cane and accompanied by two fellow officers, Jack Tatum was led from the car into the station. After two weeks in the hospital, the last thing Jack wanted was a party. He was still a long way from fine. He was hoping for a quiet send off, but the chances of that were slim to none. The cops were known for loud ceremonious retirement parties for their comrades injured in the line of duty. It was a "there, but for the grace of God go I" celebration.

He missed Eddie Mozhinsky's funeral. He missed the release of the mob. He learned that Stanley Wolfson went on stress leave and they did not know when and if he would return to duty. He heard that Mitchell Landau was arrested for conspiracy to commit murder. All this in two weeks. Seemed more like a year. And none of it made any sense. He knew Mitch. Mitch wanted the arrests and the convictions. Why would he leak Hsiao Tzu's location? Jack's thoughts were interrupted as he walked into the station to a big and loud "Surprise!"

As he anticipated, the party was a drag. Cops telling war stories, and, for some reason, each one of them feeling the need to make jokes about Jack's retirement to Palm Springs. "Got your own personal putter, there, Jack, old boy," said one cop referring to Jack's cane.

"You're a good man, Jack." Grant Bellinger approached Jack putting his hand on his shoulder. "This should never have happened."

"How did it happen, Grant?" Jack asked.

"Well, that's for the court and the jury to determine now. Landau will stand trial for sure."

"Why would he do it? That's what I don't understand." Jack pressed.

"To get at me, of course. He wanted me to take the blame for the leak. He knew that it would be the D.A., not the assistant D.A. that would ultimately take the blame. 'The buck stops here,' as the saying goes. I announced the arrests to the press and I would have to take the heat from the press announcing the release of these criminals."

"I never figured Mitch for a killer, though."

"Oh, Jack. Sometimes it's just hard to figure who is and who isn't. Political ambition can change a person. But not to worry. The election is only ten days away, and Landau's little plot failed."

"Grant, I did want to ask you. What happened to that George Stone character? Was he released too?"

"Stone . . . Stone . . . Which one was he? Sorry, there were so many."

"White collar criminal guy, older, balding."

"Sorry, Jack, I just don't remember. Thanks to Landau, the only one we were able to keep was Da Matzu because he was independently nailed by the bank people in a lineup. Well, good luck to you, Jack. Sorry to lose such a fine cop, but you sure deserve the rest." Bellinger gave Jack a perfunctory handshake and walked away.

When the party was over, Jack Tatum sat alone at his desk emptying the contents of the drawers into a cardboard box. Eighteen years on the force without ever firing his weapon. Eighteen years on the streets without getting so much as a mark on him. And then to be almost killed in some sinister political plot ostensibly perpetrated by one of his own. A strange twist, he thought, and one that just did not compute. In the many years as a detective, Jack developed that keen sense for logical explanations as well as a great need for closure. He had handled hundreds of cases, and none of them went cold. He could hardly let this one go there.

As he placed the last few items in the box, he reached into his shirt pocket. There was the business card holder with "Tess Lowe" engraved on it and a bullet hole through the middle. With all the training and on the job experience, he owed his life to this stranger. He stared at the business card holder for a while and then called his wife.

"There's one more thing I have to do here, dear. I'll be home soon. Yes. I feel fine. Don't worry."

The Stranger

The rains seemed endless in New Orleans. Charlie Parks was getting restless. He hadn't heard from George and he was not permitted to call him. He was running low on cash but was afraid to touch the money in his accounts in case there was a problem and the transaction could be traced. When the sky cleared momentarily, Charlie walked over to the post office in the hopes that his refund had arrived.

He found two envelopes inside his mail box. One he was expecting. The other was blank. Charlie opened the marked envelope and found a check for $1,500.00 made payable to Sean Masters. Pursuant to their agreement, Mel kept $500.00 under the table for keeping quiet about Charlie's location. "Lady troubles," Charlie had explained to Mel who was very understanding and willing to do just about anything for $500.00. Inside the unmarked envelope, Charlie found a typed note:

"Tuesday night, 8:00 PM, at the Third Street Bar and Grill."

"It's about time," Charlie thought.

The Third Street Bar and Grill was crowded and loud even on a Wednesday night. Charlie, wearing gray pants and a cotton black shirt, sat down at the bar and ordered a Budweiser. He stared at the TV above the bar, and periodically checked his watch. At 8:15 PM, he heard a voice next to his ear.

"Budweiser? I would think with the money you stole you could afford imported beer."

Startled, Charlie turned to face the voice addressing him.

"Jesus," he exclaimed under his breath.

"No. The name is Tess, not Jesus. I am sensing that you are ever so slightly surprised to see me. Don't look around." Tess said as Charlie was panning the room. "I didn't bring the cops. Yet."

"Tess. I don't know what to say."

"You can start by telling me where the money is. Not just mine, but Jim's and Milly's. After that you can tell me all about your pal Walter Manning or should I call him George Stone."

"How the hell do you know this? And how did you find me?"

"That's not important. I am here to get back every last dime you stole from me and my friends. My strong resolve should not be an issue. I am here, and that should tell you everything."

Charlie was silent. He could not think. He had to think. He slowly drank his beer in the hopes that his brain would start functioning again.

"Do you know that two people are dead because of your friend Stone? One a cop and one a witness who would have nailed Stone and the Chinese mafia. Another cop almost died." Tess was guessing about Stone's involvement. But two people did die and Jack Tatum was wounded, and Stone went free. This was enough of a connection.

"What are you talking about, Tess? You're talking crazy."

Tess shoved two editions of *The L.A. Times* in front of Charlie. One headlined the murder of Hsiao Tzu and the release of the mafia. The other, more recent, talked about the bail hearing of Mitchell Landau.

"I've heard this on the news, but what does this have to do with me or Stone?"

"He was arrested along with the mob. I saw him on TV and recognized him as Walter Manning, one of your so-called investors. He was arrested with the mob and released along with them. Don't tell me this is news to you."

It was news to Charlie.

"I'm waiting." Tess said.

"Not here." Charlie answered rolling up the newspapers and putting them under his arm. They left the Third Street Bar and Grill and walked.

"Who else knows about The Oregon Project?" Charlie asked.

"What difference does that make?"

"Tess, look, I never meant to hurt you. I . . ."

"The hell you didn't. You targeted me from the start. You showed up at my gallery, flirted with me, denied that our relationship had anything to do with The Oregon Project. You came to my house, Charlie. We made love. Or, should I say, you fucked me. Literally and figuratively.

"But forget about me. Do you have any idea what you did to Jim? You stole his retirement money. And Milly. Her father left that money to her so that she would be financially secure. Funny, how that worked. He left it in trust so that Milly wouldn't get it until she was mature enough to spend it wisely, and look what happened. You are the worst kind of thief, Charlie. At least those who rip off your purse or wallet on the street don't pretend to be any-thing else but thieves. You lull people into a false sense of secu-rity. You not only steal their money, you steal their trust, their sense of self-worth. You change the course of their lives in ways you can hardly imagine."

"I don't have the money." Charlie said.

"Bullshit. You didn't do this for your health. You got a big portion of the money."

"I got a portion of it, yes. But, between my apartment, furniture, and the last month of travel, I don't have much left."

"You just don't quit, do you. The furniture was rented and so was the apartment. I guess I'm just going to let the cops deal with this." Tess turned around and began walking away.

"Wait. Tess. Wait." Charlie went after her. "Look, no more lies. O.K.? I'm just scared that my partner won't take this lying down, especially being in this mess." Charlie said pointing to the newspa-pers still under his arm. "So, I'm just trying to think of a way to get your money back without giving away that it was me."

"You selfish son of a bitch. You're still thinking only of yourself. I don't give a shit whether you get hurt in the process. Why should I? Let me make this very clear to you. You only have two options. You tell me where the money is or you tell the cops."

"How about a third option?" Charlie asked.

"Such as?"

"Let's walk."

CHAPTER

The Phone Call

The sun set and George grabbed his beach towel and headed to his villa. Inside, he showered, shaved, and ordered room service. The phone rang and George picked it up.

"One moment, sir, please," said the operator.

"George, can you hear me? It's Reggie."

"Yes, Reggie, I can hear you. We have a good connection."

"I think I have a buyer for you."

"That's great news, Reggie."

"Yeah, except it's an unusual situation, and I need to discuss it with you."

"How unusual?" George asked.

"Well, first, the good news. He'll pay the asking price of $1.3 million and he'll pay cash."

"You're right. That is unusual. What's the bad news?"

"Well, I am dealing through his lawyer. The lawyer says that his client is Saudi and in the oil business. Money means nothing to this guy and that's why he'll pay the asking price without haggling. But, he won't buy the property without meeting you personally and he doesn't trust escrow companies. Won't put his money into escrow.

It's a cash transaction. He will meet you with the cashier's check and exchange it for the deed. The other thing is that privacy is extremely important to him and he will not give his name until the deal is going through. He wants the deed prepared in every respect but the name. When you get the cashier's check, you'll fill out the name as it appears on the check."

"This sounds weird, Reggie. Have you met his lawyer?"

"I did. The guy came into my office."

"What did he look like?"

"He looked like a lawyer. How else do I describe him? He was young, attractive, dressed well."

"Do they know where I am?" George asked.

"Of course, not. You were very specific about that."

"Where does he want to meet?"

"The lawyer said that did not matter. The Saudi likes the house a lot. It's perfect for his needs and, from what the lawyer tells me, his client is an impulse buyer. Of course, they say that the impulses don't last long, and the deal must be done within a week, or it's off. So what do you want me to tell them, George?"

"All right, Reggie. Let's do this. Tell him we'll set up a meeting in Bangkok. Set it up for this Sunday at the Sukhotai Hotel. Call their business office and reserve a board room for two o'clock. Federal Express the deed to me, Reggie. Prepare it except for the buyer's name and my signature. I'll sign it here and have it notarized."

"I'll do that, George, and I hope it bloody works. It's certainly the strangest deal I've ever worked on. Well, anyway, I'll call you to let you know that it is all set up. Stay well."

The Preliminary Hearing

"All rise and face the flag." The bailiff ordered as the full courtroom rose in unison and turned their torsos to face the symbol. "The Honorable Judge Betty Spenser presiding. Please be seated."

It was Thursday morning, 10:00 AM. Betty Spencer took the bench to preside over the preliminary hearing for the assistant district attorney, Mitchell Landau, charged with conspiracy to commit murder. After twenty years on the bench, Spencer developed a keen sense of truth and an even keener sense of bullshit. This, she knew without a doubt, was in the latter category. Unfortunately, she could not simply disregard the allegations or she could be accused of an appearance of impropriety and favoritism. She was here to go through the motions, but that too was part of the legal system.

"Counsel, state your appearances for the record, please." Spencer said.

"Lance Wenke, for the prosecution, Your Honor." Wenke rose to address the court.

"Jackson Boyd for the defendant, Your Honor."

"Are the People ready to proceed with the preliminary hearing, Mr. Wenke?" Spencer asked.

"We are, Your Honor."

"Mr. Boyd? Is the defense ready?"

"Yes, Your Honor."

"Very well. Mr. Wenke, call your first witness."

"People call Detective Stanley Wolfson to the stand."

Wolfson took the witness stand. He took the oath and swallowed from the cup of water placed in front of him. Under direct examination by Wenke, Wolfson painfully recounted that night in Santa Barbara. He described how he and Eddie Mozhinsky were assigned to guard Hsiao Tzu. How Jack Tatum unexpectedly came up to check on them. How he went down to the corner restaurant to get some takeout and what he found when he returned. He was sub-dued and obviously still unnerved by the events of that night.

"I saw Eddie on the floor with blood all around him. I saw the para-medics next to Jack and I saw the Little Pig lying face down with two bullet holes in the back of his head. One of the killers was also lying down next to Eddie. He was also dead."

"Now, Detective Wolfson," Wenke continued, "other than Eddie Mozhinsky, did you tell anyone else, anyone else at all about your assignment that night or where you were going to be?"

"Of course, not." Wolfson answered. "No one was supposed to know. No one."

"No further questions." Wenke concluded.

"Mr. Boyd. Cross." Judge Spencer directed the proceedings.

"Detective. I know this is hard for you, so I'll be brief." Jackson began. "You said that you did not tell anyone about your assign-ment. Who gave you your assignment?"

"Well, we were in Mr. Bellinger's office. Jack was there and Eddie, of course, and me, and Mr. Landau. Mr. Bellinger gave us the assignment."

"So, would it be correct to say that Mr. Bellinger was one of the people who knew about the assignment and the location."

Lance Wenke shot a nasty look at Jackson Boyd.

"Yes. Sure." Wolfson answered.

"Thank you, Detective. I have no further questions."

Wenke called Jack Tatum to the stand next. The same events were recounted, and the same question was posed. No, Jack did not dis-cuss the location with anyone outside of the group that was in Bel-linger's office when the directive was given.

"Mr. Boyd. Do you wish to question this witness?" Judge Spencer asked.

"Not at this time, Your Honor, but I will reserve my right to recall him." Jackson answered.

"Very well. Anything else, Mr. Wenke?" Spencer queried.

"Yes. People call Mr. Grant Bellinger to the stand."

"Wait a minute. Counsel approach." Spencer commanded. "Let me get this straight, Mr. Wenke," Spencer said when the lawyers approached the bench. "Your last witness will be Mr. Bellinger who will testify that he did not order the killing and did not reveal the information to anyone. If that's all you've got, Counsel, I am inclined to dismiss the case now and save the spectacle."

"Well, Your Honor, if you are so inclined . . ." Wenke began. He was about to achieve exactly what he was sent in to accomplish. Bellinger told him to make this quick and painless. Wenke understood. This was far from brain surgery. The goal was to leave Landau under a cloud of suspicion. An acquittal at trial would remove that cloud. But a judge, one that Landau appeared before many times, bound by the parameters of the law, finding that there was simply insufficient evidence to proceed to trial—well, that's just perfect. One could easily spin to claim that Landau not only committed the crime but was such a criminal mastermind that he left no tracks. He could see himself interviewed on Court TV.

"We want the spectacle, Judge." Jackson stated firmly.

"What?" Spencer and Wenke said almost in unison.

"We want Bellinger to take the stand, Your Honor. If you dismiss the charges now, the press will simply say that the judge dismissed the case for insufficient evidence. That's just not good enough, and my client's career will be over. They started this. Let's finish it."

Wenke was stunned. Having Spencer dismiss the charges before Bellinger testified was the best possible scenario. Bellinger never takes the stand, never has to be cross-examined, but still gets reelected.

"Very well. Proceed. But I'm giving you a short leash strictly for purposes of completeness of the record." Spencer said.

The lawyers walked back to their counsel tables. Boyd said something to Mitch while Wenke turned around and winked at Bellinger.

"The People call Mr. Grant Bellinger to the stand." Wenke announced half standing up.

Bellinger strode confidently to the witness stand and took the oath. He would tell the truth. The truth according to him.

"Mr. Bellinger. You are the district attorney, are you not?" Wenke asked the foundational question.

"Yes. I am."

"Did you, along with Detective Jack Tatum, order two police officers to protect a crucial prosecution witness by the name of Hsiao Tzu, also known as 'The Little Pig'?"

"I did. We had plea bargained with the witness and he was about to give very important testimony against the members of a Chinese cartel who had been arrested the night before." Bellinger punctuated each letter of each word as if to assure that the court reporter and the newspaper reporters did not misspell anything he said or, worse, miss it.

"Officers Mozhinsky and Wolfson were ordered to transport the witness to an undisclosed location, a motel in Santa Barbara," Bellinger continued, "and stay with him 'round the clock until he testified. After that, Hsiao Tzu was scheduled to serve a short reduced sentence and then enter our witness protection program. We had great hopes for his testimony. We would have put ten, maybe twelve, mafia hoods behind bars with him on the stand. But, he was killed."

"Besides you, Detective Jack Tatum, and the two officers, who was the only other person present in your office when those orders were given?" Wenke queried.

"Mr. Landau. Mr. Mitchell Landau. The defendant." Bellinger savored these words as Mitchell's anger smoldered inside.

"Mr. Bellinger. Did you, at any time, disclose to anyone outside your office that night, the location of the witness?"

"Absolutely not." Bellinger replied.

"No further questions, Your Honor." Wenke said.

"Very well. Counsel, are you sure you wish to proceed at this point?" Judge Spencer glanced down at Jackson Boyd, and then at Mitchell Landau.

"Oh yes, Your Honor." Boyd rose to his feet.

"Good morning, Mr. Bellinger." He addressed the D.A.

Bellinger nodded.

Boyd placed his briefcase on the table in front of him and reached in. He retrieved a manila envelope that appeared to have been filled with a rectangular object. He held it up high, and said, "May I approach the witness, Your Honor?"

"You may." The judge replied.

Boyd walked up to Bellinger. He carefully and deliberately placed the envelope on the edge of the witness stand and walked back to the counsel table. He stood there for two minutes, completely stationary and absolutely silent.

Bellinger stared at the envelope, then at Boyd and then at Wenke. What the hell was in it, he thought? What is Boyd trying to pull. This was supposed to be simple and straightforward. He'd get on the stand, testify on direct examination, keep the same story on cross-examination. Spencer would dismiss the charges for lack of evidence, but Landau's career would be immersed in suspicion and speculation over these murders. Bellinger would win the election and things would be right back where they were before Landau decided to challenge him. It was supposed to be that simple. What the hell was in this envelope?

"Are you planning on vocalizing something, Mr. Boyd?" Spencer broke the silence.

Satisfied with the duration of the silence and the focal point on the envelope, Boyd began his cross-examination.

"Mr. Bellinger. Do you know a man by the name of George Stone?"

"Objection, Your Honor," Wenke protested. "What is the relevance of this?"

"The relevance will become crystal clear in a short while, Your Honor." Boyd explained.

"Proceed. The objection is overruled. The witness will answer the question."

"If I recall correctly," Bellinger was hedging his bets, growing increasingly uneasy, "Mr. Stone was one of the people arrested in our sweep."

"What was he arrested for?"

"I believe it was for illegal business transactions."

"Did you know Mr. Stone before his arrest?"

"I don't recall hearing of him before, Mr. Boyd."

"I did not ask whether you heard of him, Mr. Bellinger. I asked whether you knew Mr. Stone before the arrest?"

Bellinger glanced anxiously at the envelope and then at Wenke as if pleading for him to stop this. Wenke shrugged his shoulders. His objection had been overruled and he had done what he could. Bellinger was on his own.

"I don't recall." Bellinger answered.

"Well, maybe this will refresh your recollection." Bellinger headed purposefully towards the witness stand and the envelope. Oh my God, Bellinger thought. The tape. But he couldn't have it. It was erased, destroyed, disposed of. He watched Boyd reach for the envelope, and then, watched him freeze, staring directly into Bellinger's eyes. Bellinger could have sworn he saw Boyd crack a smile. Then, in the same polished fashion, Boyd reversed direction, and headed back to the counsel table, saying on the way, with his back to the witness:

"Before I attempt to refresh your recollection with the contents of the envelope, Mr. Bellinger, let me ask you this. Did you hold a fund-raiser shortly before these arrests were made."

"Yes. A dinner was held in my honor to assist me in raising funds for my campaign."

"Where was that fund-raiser held?"

"Your Honor, is this going somewhere? Where Mr. Bellinger's fund-raiser was held is clearly irrelevant to this hearing," Wenke objected.

"I am growing impatient with this, Mr. Boyd. You better get somewhere soon." Judge Spencer stated.

"Isn't it true, Mr. Bellinger, that your campaign fund-raiser was held at the house of Mr. George Stone who was later arrested for illegal real estate schemes and let go after the only witness who could finger him was killed?"

The courtroom erupted with the noise of cameras and scandalous whispers. Wenke sunk in his chair, but Bellinger was only mildly phased. He expected that they might ask him this for effect, but, without the tape, they could not prove it. He simply needed to gather his composure, dismiss these accusations as ridiculous, and point the finger back at Landau for smearing a long and illustrious career.

"I am sorry, Mr. Boyd." Bellinger began. "As you may know, I am an extremely busy person. I work sixteen hours a day seven days a week putting criminals behind bars, and I've been doing this for fifteen years. It is difficult to do all this and run a campaign, but, frankly, the people of this fine city have given me thumbs up three times. Notwithstanding, to make sure that my focus is on the business of the people, I hired a campaign manager, Timothy Newsome.

"He arranged for fund-raisers and I appeared at them. I would certainly hope that Mr. Stone was not one of the people giving fund-raisers for me, and, of course, if he had made any contributions to my campaign, they should be immediately returned. But I assure you, if what you are saying is true, I had no idea." As Bellinger finished his answer, he took one more furtive glance at the envelope in front of him. It was a calculated risk, but they could not possibly have the tape. He made sure of that. This was just part of the Jackson Boyd theater, and he was too experienced to fall for it.

"I have no further questions at this time, Your Honor, but we reserve our right to recall Mr. Bellinger." Boyd declared.

"Counsel, one more time to the bench, please." Judge Spencer motioned to the lawyers. As Wenke and Boyd made their way to the bench, Spencer said,

"Counsel, I will not permit the use of my courtroom and the public funds to be wasted on your campaign shenanigans. I am going to dismiss this case and you folks do whatever you want to do on TV and *Meet the Press*. I don't care. But this is getting ridiculous, and I won't have it."

"The prosecution understands your decision, Your Honor." Wenke said.

"The defense begs to differ. Look, Judge, if you are truly interested in the productive use of your courtroom and honest use of public funds, give me one more hour and two more witnesses."

"To what end?" Spencer inquired.

"Murder, Your Honor, and who did it."

"What?" Wenke swallowed hard. "What the hell is that supposed to mean?"

"Yes, Counsel, where are you going with this?"

"Two witnesses, Your Honor, that's all I ask. They got their preliminary hearing with no evidence. They got the press to print that my client was charged with murder. Please. Two witnesses."

"He's got a point, Counsel." Spencer addressed Wenke. "Your theatrics with this case were not lost on me. You brought this case against an assistant D.A. with no evidence and during a heated election. You must take me for a fool if you think I don't get it. On the other hand. Two wrongs don't make a right. You've got one hour and two witnesses, Mr. Boyd. After that, I dismiss the case, and go home to watch the fireworks on CNN. Got it?"

"Your Honor . . ." Wenke protested.

"That's all, Counsel. Now, the court will recess for lunch. When we return this afternoon, we'll have the two witnesses. That's it."

The Transaction

Sitting alone at the conference room at the Sukhotai Hotel two days later, George was reviewing the grant deed he was about to sign over to a Saudi. A stranger was going to live in his home, sleep in his bedroom, eat in his dining room. He hated the thought, but he had no choice. The door opened and in came a handsome young man dressed in a business suit carrying a briefcase.

"Mr. Stone?" Asked the handsome stranger.

"Yes. And you are?"

"That's not important. My client is prepared to complete the business transaction." The man put the briefcase on the table. "Did you bring the deed?"

"Yes." George said. "Did you bring the cashier's check?"

The lawyer took a cashier's check out of his briefcase. "$1.3 million made payable to Vincent Taylor as you requested. Where is the deed?"

George took out the deed from the envelope and placed it on the table.

"Who do I make the proud new owner of my home?"

"Just make the deed out to Res Ipsa Loquitur Foundation—my client's business enterprise. I assume you have arranged for a notary."

George summoned the notary and gave her instructions to complete the deed and to return in order to notarize George's signature. The men were left alone.

"What kind of an organization is this Res Ipsa . . .? Sounds like a strange name for a venture owned by a Saudi oil man." George asked.

"I am not at liberty to discuss my client's business affairs, Mr. Stone. If you are hungry for information, read a newspaper."

The notary returned with the completed deed and her notary book. The transaction was complete. The lawyer walked out with the deed, and George Stone was staring at his cashier's check. All he had to do now was deposit the money into his account at the Siam bank. Then, he just had to sit it out before returning to the U.S. and starting a new life.

The next morning, George Stone was awakened by the phone.

"Hello," he answered groggily.

"Mr. Taylor? I am very sorry to bother you."

"Who is this?"

"This is Mr. Khanh from the bank. We have a problem. Can you come to Bangkok right away?"

"What kind of problem?" George asked.

"Well, you see, sir. The American bank will not honor the cashier's check you deposited."

"What?" George sat up straight as an arrow.

"I know. This never happened before, but they say the check was typed up by someone who did not work at the bank and there were no funds paid to cover it."

"That's their fucking problem. It's a cashier's check, for God's sake. They have no choice but to honor it."

"That's what I told them, but they say that they think it's some kind of scheme and they are investigating it and they'll let us know what they find out."

"Investigating it, my ass. Who did you talk to there. Give me the name and number. I'm gonna break some heads."

"I talked to the vice president. Name is Lowe. Steven Lowe. Number is (213) 512-3425."

"Lowe. Lowe. Why the hell does that sound . . ." George felt his body temperature drop. His palms began to sweat. It couldn't be. How the hell . . . It had to be a coincidence. But more importantly, his house was now in someone else's name and he got no money for it. He dialed the number for Reggie Blair.

"Pick up the phone, damnit." George muttered angrily as the phone kept ringing.

"Hello?"

"Reggie. It's George. Listen to me."

"George. What's wrong?"

"What's wrong is that I got fucked on our real estate deal and you're going to help me get un-fucked."

"What are you talking about George. What do you mean, fucked? You said everything went fine."

"Oh, it went fine, alright, until the bank in L.A. refused to honor the cashier's check."

"They can't do that." Reggie contributed.

"I know they can't. But they said that someone just issued the check at the bank without getting funds and they are investigating it. It gets worse. And I can't tell you everything, Reggie, but if what I think happened happened, I am in serious trouble. I need your help."

"Sure, George. What can I do?"

"Call the number I'm going to give you and ask for Steven Lowe, vice president. Tell him you're my real estate agent and find out everything you can about what happened. Also, call the county recorder's office and find out if the deed has been recorded. Keep me informed about every little detail, but under no circumstances, tell them where I am. Got it?"

"I got it George."

"And remember, your big fat commission is riding on the validity of this check."

CHAPTER

Lunch Break

Bellinger pulled into his reserved parking space and headed to his office. He had one hour, one lunch break, to figure out whether Boyd was bluffing. Newsome was waiting. Bellinger closed the door behind him.

"What's going on, Newsome? What have they got? Who are their two witnesses and what the hell are they planning to do with them?"

Newsome sat silent.

"Are you listening to me?"

"I heard what you said in court about me. I did not appreciate it." Newsome finally spoke. "You made me look like a fool. No one is going to ever hire me for another campaign. I really did not appreciate that."

"Listen to me, Newsome. I did the only thing I could do when I was confronted with that situation. What would you have recommended? That I admit knowing Stone? Maybe I should admit that he contributed heavily to my campaign? Do you think you'd work after that? The bottom line is that if we win, the only thing people are going to remember is that you ran a successful campaign. If I lose, that's when they'll never hire you. I was thinking of both of us."

"I highly doubt that." Newsome retorted.

"All right. Fine. I am a selfish pig. So sue me. My ass is on the line, Newsome, or are you not clear on the concept? And, may I say, so is yours. Now, let's stop this and figure out what is going on this afternoon in that courtroom. Who do you think their two witnesses are?"

"I don't know. Do you think they've got Stone?"

"No way. And why would Stone testify anyway. No. He's long gone. What about that investigator, Murdoch?"

"I don't think so. Murdoch only participated in that one fiasco with the drunk driving. I never let him see the computer entries and he doesn't know the password."

"Why are we documenting those contributions anyway? Isn't it foolish to keep a record of illegal campaign contributions?" Bellinger asked.

"You wanted the record, Grant, so you wouldn't forget who to thank when you got reelected."

"This smells, Newsome. Boyd may be bluffing, but when those courtroom doors open after lunch, he's got to put somebody on that stand. And what good does it do anyway? Bluff me into doing what? I can't dismiss the charges, or I'll look wishy-washy. No. Threats from Kari Landau notwithstanding, the only right play is to play it out."

"With all due respect, sir, don't you think we are beyond the right play to keep you in office. Aren't we talking about murder here?" Newsome was treading cautiously.

"What are you implying, son? What are you implying?"

"That you had something to do with the rubbing out of The Little Pig." There. I said it. Newsome muttered to himself.

"Are you out of your mind?" Bellinger was fuming. "I would never murder anyone. I am not capable of murder. Landau let the location leak. He is responsible for the murder. Not me. I had nothing to do with it."

"What about what Kari said. Are you looking for the shooter who escaped? Because I'm spending virtually every hour with you, and I am not seeing any action in that regard."

"That's because that is none of your business. Your job is to reelect me, not to do my job. I've got good detectives on that."

"Whatever you say, sir." Newsome said tautly and got up to leave. "I must say. Working with you has been quite an experience."

"Where are you going?" Bellinger asked nervously.

"Don't worry, Grant. I won't make any noise to interfere with the election. Unfortunately, that's not my style. One must have courage and a clean conscience to stand up for what's right. Apparently, I have neither."

First National Bank,
the Day of the Preliminary Hearing

As soon as he hung up the phone, Reggie did as he was told. But, instead of using the telephone, he thought he would pay a personal visit to Mr. Lowe. As a salesman, he knew there was nothing like that personal touch. Besides, with his charm and his British accent, he should be able to get to the bottom of this silly problem and free up his big fat commission.

"I am here to see Mr. Steven Lowe." Reggie announced to the bank officer seated at a desk. "My name is Reggie Blair. He is expecting me. Tell him it's about the George Stone transaction. He might also know it as the Res Ipsa Loquitur Foundation transaction, if I am indeed pronouncing that correctly. That was your customer."

"Please have a seat, Mr. Blair. I'll let him know you are here." The young lady disappeared behind a wall into a back corridor. Reggie sat down, crossed his legs, and began nervously twitching his left shoulder—a habit he was unaware of.

Finally, after waiting fifteen minutes, the bank teller appeared from behind the wall and led him into a back office.

"Please wait here. Mr. Lowe will be right with you."

Five minutes later, Steven Lowe entered the room.

"Hello, Mr. Blair. I am Steven Lowe. I understand you have a message for us from Mr. Stone."

"Well, actually, I thought you might have a message for him. As you know, your bank issued a cashier's check for quite a large sum of money."

"Yes. $1.3 million." Steven said.

"Yes. And you see, his bank in Bangkok said that there is a problem honoring that check. So, I thought, I would come in and talk to you to see what can be resolved."

"It's a shame that Mr. Stone could not come personally." Steven said. "I am sure he could give us a hand in this investigation. After all, real estate schemes are his special talent."

"Whatever do you mean?" Reggie said nervously.

"Are you involved with Mr. Stone in his real estate schemes? Specifically, Mr. Blair, are you involved in The Oregon Project?" Steven pressed.

"I have no idea what you are talking about."

"And many people had no idea they were getting ripped off. Now, you came for a message, terrific, here is one. Tell Stone to forget about his house and to forget about the cashier's check. The money he used to buy that house was stolen. The house will be sold and the money will be given back to the victims of his schemes. Tell him that if he so much as squeaks or does anything to try to get the house or the money back, we will turn him into the cops so quickly his head will spin. Did you get all that, Mr. Blair, or should I repeat it?"

"I will give your message to Mr. Stone." Reggie responded, reluctantly kissing his commission goodbye.

"You do that." Steven concluded, "And next time, Mr. Blair, pick a better set of clients."

As Reggie's frame was no longer visible, Steven made a congratulatory fist. The scumbag who stole money from his baby sister had been put in his place. They were not sure whether Stone would come or call or if he would send someone. They were ready for any contingency. It really did not matter. What they knew for sure was that Stone was hardly in the position to complain to the cops, to the bank, or to anyone else. He picked up the phone to share his joy with Tess.

One Hour and Two Witnesses

It was 1:30, and Judge Spencer's courtroom was still closed to the public for the lunch break. In her chambers, Spencer took off her street coat and hung it on the coat rack. She sat down behind her desk and looked at the two lawyers who came into her chambers at her request.

"I have had an opportunity to think this whole matter over during lunch, Counsel, and I must say that I am having serious reservations about allowing you to proceed with your witnesses, Mr. Boyd. It just seems to me that this is a matter that is appropriately handled by the police and the D.A.'s office. And although I realize that this may be a difficult task for you, I still think that that is a more appropriate forum."

"Your Honor," Boyd said. "I appreciate the court's reservations and concerns. I have been before you many times and I have always respected your decisions. I know this is a highly unusual request considering the fact that you are prepared to dismiss the charges against my client. But if you do that, there is a high probability that this evidence will not come to light and certainly not in a way that it should."

"Why do you say that, Counsel. Frankly, the suspense is killing me. Do you know what he's prepared to offer, Mr. Wenke?"

"I have no idea, Your Honor." Wenke answered.

"Mr. Boyd. I would be more willing to allow you to go on this afternoon if you can make an offer of proof."

"I would be happy to do that, Your Honor, but with Mr. Wenke present, I am afraid that he will do what any lawyer would do—tell his client. I would be willing to make an offer of proof to you *in camera* and *ex-parte*."

"Your Honor, I object. This is highly unusual and completely inappropriate. *In camera* hearings are reserved for extremely sensitive matters for the judge's eyes only, and *ex-parte*, Your Honor, excluding me, well, that's highly prejudicial. It is one thing if a jury is making a decision, and you are simply involved in admitting or disallowing evidence, Judge, but you are the person making the decision. I strenuously object." Wenke protested.

"That's true, Counsel. But I am also the person who has already made the decision against you, and you are anxious to accept it. Don't you think that's unusual? This whole thing is unusual, Counsel, and you and your boss, Mr. Wenke, put me in this position. So, what's your point. You plan on appealing a decision you desire so greatly? I will receive the offer of proof as requested by Mr. Boyd. Now, please go into the courtroom and leave us alone."

Wenke reluctantly left Spencer's chambers and walked through the hall separating the chambers from the courtroom. He walked in through the back door by the judge's bench over to his counsel table where Bellinger was waiting impatiently.

"What the hell is going on, Wenke," Bellinger snapped. "Why are they still in there?"

"Boyd is making an offer of proof on this afternoon's witnesses *in camera*."

"What do you mean he's making an offer of proof *in camera*. What kind of crap is that?"

At that moment, Wenke and Bellinger saw the judge's door to the courtroom open. Boyd headed for his side of the courtroom. They tried to read his face, but it was expressionless. Boyd did not sit down. He put down his briefcase and stood behind the counsel table with Mitch by his side. Within seconds, Judge Spencer, wearing her black robe garb, walked out and sat behind the judge's bench. She acknowledged Boyd and briefly glanced at Wenke and Bellinger.

The courtroom remained silent for what seemed forever as the parties and the judge waited for the court reporter to appear from her office and take a seat.

"Mr. Bailiff, please open the courtroom," Judge Spencer ordered. "Let's proceed."

The courtroom filled quickly and fell silent immediately. Boyd and Landau took their places at their counsel table. Wenke sat at his. Bellinger took a seat in the first row. After all, he reasoned, he was not the prosecutor on this case, just a witness. At this moment he wished he was neither.

"Mr. Bellinger, please retake the witness stand, and remember that you are still under oath."

"Certainly, Your Honor," Bellinger tried to maintain as he sunk into the witness chair.

"Proceed with your examination, Mr. Boyd." Spencer ordered.

"I have only one more question for this witness, Your Honor. Mr. Bellinger, I want you to think carefully when you answer this question. Isn't it true that it was you, not Mitch Landau, who leaked the location of government witness, Hsiao Tzu?"

The courtroom erupted. Wenke objected. Spencer banged her gavel and ordered silence.

"How dare you imply that I . . ." Bellinger protested.

"It's a yes or no question, Mr. Bellinger," Boyd interrupted.

"No. A thousand times 'No.'" Bellinger answered.

"Thank you, Mr. Bellinger. I'm done with this witness, Judge."

"You may step down, Mr. Bellinger. But don't you go anywhere." Judge Spencer said.

With a lonely bead of sweat hanging on his eyebrow, Bellinger stepped down and wobbled to his seat. He no longer believed that this was a game of chicken. They had something, or someone. But this had to be played out. This would be played out.

"Your Honor, the defense recalls Detective Jack Tatum." Boyd announced.

Judge Spencer motioned to the bailiff to get the next witness from the hall as witnesses were excluded from the courtroom. Within a minute, the double doors swung open and Detective Jack Tatum walked in. He was used to testifying in court. It had became second nature to him. But this was different. This was special. Jack walked up to the witness chair and took the oath. He sat down and took a sip of water.

"You may proceed," Spencer motioned to Jackson Boyd.

"Good afternoon, Detective,"

"Good afternoon, Counsel."

"Detective, as part of your investigation into this matter, did you have occasion to inspect a particular computer file?"

"I did."

"Would you please describe for us what you discovered."

"Your Honor, this is highly inappropriate." Wenke jumped. "I demand an offer of proof. I have no way of defending my client without knowing about the evidence they are about to introduce."

"Did you misspeak, Mr. Wenke?" Judge Spencer said. "I thought your clients were the People of the State of California, and I also thought that you were the prosecuting attorney, not the defense attorney. Now, do you still have an objection you wish for me to rule on?"

"Withdrawn, Your Honor." Wenke said sullenly.

"You may continue, Detective," Spencer addressed Jack Tatum.

"I have never been comfortable with the turn of events in this case." Jack began. "I've known Mitch Landau for many years, and I just couldn't fathom that he would have any role in a murder. So, one night, on a hunch you could say, I went into Mr. Bellinger's office just to look around. I mean that was the place where we all got together and discussed the Little Pig and where he was going to be, and I thought maybe something would jump out at me, something that could help me understand what really happened. And as I sat in that room, I saw the computer and I just instinctively turned it on. It took me some time to get into the system because it needed a password, but I finally cracked it. I don't know how I guessed it, but somehow it came to me."

That night after his retirement party, Jack sat at his desk and made notes on his note pad. He did this routinely when he was confronted with a complicated case. On the left side, in a vertical column, he listed things he knew. On the right side, he wrote down things he wanted to know. Somehow having the two sides staring at each other made things make sense. Sometimes.

On the left side of his note pad, he wrote down the name Tess Lowe. Underneath, he wrote the name George Stone. He connected the two names by a dollar sign. Stone ran illegal schemes. He stole money and, most likely, had been doing this for years. But he never got caught. Why not? Was he that careful or did someone look the other way?

On the right side of the note pad, Jack Tatum wrote down three names. Hsiao Tzu, Mitchell Landau, and Grant Bellinger. He put a line through Hsiao Tzu's name and a question mark next to Landau. He stared at the page for a long time. A strange mix of characters, wasn't it? The district attorney and his assistant fighting each other for the office, on the same page as two criminals and a victim of grand theft. Many people wanted Hsiao Tzu dead, but who leaked his location? Jack circled Bellinger's name and then Stone's. What was the connection?

He looked around the office. It was empty and would be until morning. He stood up from his desk and headed across the street to Bellinger's office. He didn't know what he was looking for, but he wasn't going to find it at his own desk.

When he got to the offices housing the district attorneys, he walked up to the guard and smiled,

"Hey, Sam. How's it going?"

"It's going. What brings you here this late? Word has it you picked up your gold watch on the way to Palm Springs?"

"Just tying up some loose ends." Jack said as he walked by Sam and disappeared down the corridor.

Bellinger's office was clean as usual. There were several piles of papers on his desk, but nothing out of the ordinary. He sat in Bellinger's chair behind his desk and swiveled back and forth waiting for clues to pop into his head.

Jack swung the chair to face Bellinger's computer and turned it on. The computer prompted for a password. So much for this idea, Jack thought. There is no way to get into this damn thing without a password and that could be any word or words of ten letters or less. What's the number of those possibilities? Must be in the thousands.

Jack typed in the word "asshole" and pushed the return button. The computer responded with "Improper password. Try again?" Jack examined the office as if the password was going to pop into his head magically.

"Oh, what the hell. Let's try a few." Jack muttered to himself and typed in his next try: "attorney." Again, the computer rejected it. He tried "Bellinger," "verdict," "trial," "campaign," but nothing worked. He shuffled through the papers on Bellinger's desk, again spying for clues, but with no success. Jack was ready to give up until he remembered something he overheard a few months ago.

"And what was that password, Detective?" Boyd asked.

"Dinosaur. It was 'dinosaur,' a term I heard used in reference to Mr. Bellinger. I guess he decided to adopt it for himself in his password."

"And what did you discover when you punched in that password?"

"I got a list of files on the screen. One of them was called 'Contributions.' I printed the contents of that file."

"Did you bring that with you?" Boyd asked.

"I did." Jack Tatum opened an envelope and took out a two-page document.

"Would you please describe for us the contents of that document."

"It appears to be a list of names of contributors to Grant Bellinger's reelection campaign and the amounts they contributed."

"Objection, Your Honor," Wenke stood up. "Judge, we are here only to determine whether there is enough evidence to hold Mr. Landau over for trial. This is far afield of anything even closely resembling that purpose."

"Overruled." Spencer said.

"But, Your Honor," Wenke resisted.

"Counsel, your objection is not well taken. You opened the door. I'm just letting them walk through it." Spencer stated poignantly.

"And does one of those names match the name of one of the suspects arrested in the Chinese mafia sweep?" Boyd continued.

"Yes."

"And what name is that, Detective?"

"There is a reference here to a George Stone with a contribution amount of $50,000.00. Mr. Stone was one of the people we arrested. He was charged with criminal fraud for perpetrating numerous real estate and other schemes and taking many people for a lot of money."

"Thank you, Detective," Boyd Jackson concluded. "Your witness," he said to Lance Wenke.

"Detective Tatum," Wenke rose to his feet to cross-examine the witness. "Did you have a search warrant to search Mr. Bellinger's computer?"

"I did not."

"Did you have any probable cause, any immediate, urgent need to search Mr. Bellinger's computer without having enough time to get a search warrant?"

"I was concerned that the information could be erased by the time I got the search warrant." Jack Tatum answered.

"Detective, isn't it true that you didn't even know if there was anything on that computer when you went in to search it—you were just fishing?"

"I had reason to believe that . . ."

"Can you answer my question, yes or no."

"Yes, it's true."

"Your Honor," Wenke began. "This was clearly an illegal search and this evidence simply cannot come in. There was no warrant and no probable cause for a warrantless search."

"And your point being what, Mr. Wenke, that I should not consider this evidence in determining whether this case should proceed to trial?"

Wenke realized that he was had. Of course this would not proceed to trial and who cares if this comes into evidence. His boss was just clobbered and he just made a fool of himself. He looked over at Bellinger who was red-faced and grinding his jaw. Wenke composed himself.

"May I continue," Wenke asked the judge.

"Knock yourself out, Counsel," Judge Spencer said.

"Detective, do you know who put that information into the computer?"

"I do not."

"Do you know when it was put into the computer?"

"I do not."

"You can't even tell us whether Mr. Bellinger had anything to do with these entries, can you?"

"It was in his computer and a password was required, so we can assume . . ."

"I did not ask you to assume, sir, I asked you whether you knew, for a fact, that Mr. Bellinger had anything to do with these entries."

"I can't tell you that for a fact."

"Thank you. No further questions, Your Honor." Wenke was quite pleased with himself and glanced at his boss for approval. It wasn't there.

"Anything else for this witness, Mr. Boyd?"

"No, Your Honor."

"You may step down, Detective, with thanks from the court." Jack stepped down from the witness chair and, with the assistance of his cane, walked back to his seat in the audience. As he looked up, he noticed a familiar face. Tess Lowe, the woman who unwittingly saved his life was sitting among the courtroom crowd showering him with a warm smile.

"Thank you," Jack mouthed to her.

"No, thank you." She responded in kind.

"You have another witness, Mr. Boyd?"

"Yes, Your Honor." Boyd signaled to the bailiff to bring the next witness from the hall. As the bailiff proceeded out of the court-room, there was absolute silence. No one spoke. No one moved. No one took notes. All heads turned to the heavy double doors.

Only three people in the courtroom knew who was on the other side of these double doors, and they too were silent and mesmerized by the intensity of the moment.

When the doors swung open, the bailiff reentered the courtroom and proceeded to his desk. No one followed him and the doors closed behind him. For a brief moment, Bellinger felt immense relief that Jackson Boyd's mystery witness failed to appear. It was then that the double doors opened again. The witness arrived. He walked past the sitting crowd of observers whose heads followed him as he headed towards the witness stand intently and deliberately. There was no hesitation in his manner as he stood by the witness stand prepared to take the oath.

"Do you swear to tell the truth, the whole truth and nothing but the truth?"

"I do." The witness said and sat down prepared to testify.

"Would you state your full name for the record." Jackson asked.

"Yes. My name is Timothy Layne Newsome, Jr." Newsome stared directly at Bellinger.

"Mr. Newsome. You are Mr. Bellinger's campaign manager?"

"Was. I have resigned."

Jackson retrieved an envelope from his briefcase that looked identical to the one with which he had previously taunted Bellinger.

"Your Honor, the defense would like to mark this envelope and its contents as Defense Exhibit 1."

"So marked." Spencer responded.

"Mr. Newsome," Boyd continued, "did you provide me with the contents of this envelope?"

"Yes, I did."

"Your Honor, may I approach the witness?"

"Yes, Counsel." Spencer approved.

Jackson walked up to the witness stand and handed Newsome the envelope. He turned to face Bellinger sitting in the front row. As he was finished as a witness, he was permitted to stay in the court-room. Besides, neither side wanted him excluded and would say nothing about his presence.

Jackson had many prior dealings with Bellinger in their long paral-lel careers. He understood and believed that they each had a func-tion in this system, and each of them had to do things he may personally dislike. But Jackson always thought of them as soldiers. Not the way many people challenged their professions by pointing in disgust to the German soldiers during World War II who excused their cowardly atrocities with lack of free will akin to ants in a col-ony, moving unwaveringly with the crowd, as if there were no choice in their lot in life. No. That comparison was too simple, and as wrong as the self-righteous ramblings of those lawyers who pre-tended that they were part of some higher moral ground.

Jackson saw himself, and Bellinger for that matter, as soldiers in a system that worked most of the time. Plain and simple. The best system in the world. Not perfect, mind you, because perfection was not an option when the players were human. Nor was perfec-tion necessary.

But the system worked only if the ground rules were followed. The basic parameters within which many things were possible and even more things acceptable. But not this. Bellinger crossed the line in a way that made a farce of the system. A system that Jackson strongly believed in. He told Bellinger as much as he looked at him, standing next to Newsome and the envelope.

"Mr. Newsome. Would you please remove the contents of the envelope and identify them for this court." Boyd requested, walk-ing back to his counsel table so that the witness had the floor and that his actions were clearly visible. Newsome reached inside the envelope and removed a small cassette tape.

"This tape contains the confession of Hsiao Tzu when Mr. Landau interrogated him. I removed it from the evidence room on direct orders from Mr. Bellinger who told me to get it and destroy it because it implicated him."

Bellinger rested his head in his hands. Reporters were feverishly writing notes.

"Why didn't you destroy it, Mr. Newsome?" Boyd asked.

"Frankly, I didn't want even to take it from the evidence room. It was obviously illegal. But, all my life, I've been spineless, and followed orders, and this was no exception. But I just couldn't go as far as destroying evidence. I was hoping that this whole thing would just resolve itself, and the tape would become irrelevant. But when I realized that we were talking about murder, I couldn't be a part of it."

"Your Honor, at this time, we request that the tape be admitted into evidence, and played for the record." Jackson stated.

"Objection, Your Honor." Wenke was looking for a miracle. "Look, Judge, even if what this witness is saying is accepted by this court, which it clearly should not be, Mr. Newsome cannot authenticate this tape. Further, what is contained on it is hearsay. It's clearly an out of court statement by someone who is dead, submitted to prove that what he is saying is true. It's textbook hearsay."

"Counsel?" Spencer turned to Boyd.

"He's right, Judge." Boyd announced. "But the tape falls into an exception."

"Such as?" Spencer asked.

"The tape has independent significance. It's submitted to bolster this witness's credibility and to explain why Mr. Bellinger would want the tape erased. As such, even if what Mr. Hsiao said on it is not true, the fact that he said it and Mr. Bellinger wanted it deleted has significance of its own, independent of the hearsay statements."

"The objection is overruled." Spencer decided. "The tape is admitted into evidence. You may play it for the record, Counsel."

"That won't be necessary." Said a voice from the front row.

Bellinger stood up from the crowd and walked over to the judge's bench. The bailiff immediately ran up to him.

"It's O.K." Spencer motioned to the bailiff. "You wish to speak with me, Mr. Bellinger?"

"Yes, Your Honor." Bellinger responded in a virtual whisper.

"Go wait for me in my chambers." She ordered. "I have some business to attend to first."

As Bellinger, accompanied by the bailiff, shuffled to the judge's chambers, he heard Judge Spencer say "This court finds that there is insufficient evidence to hold this defendant over for trial. The case is dismissed. Mr. Landau, you are free to go."

Mitch jumped to his feet and hugged Jackson. Many times adversaries, they were now closer than most good friends. They accomplished everything they set out to do. Unlike most of his victories, Jackson Boyd knew that in this case justice prevailed and he helped make it happen. It felt great.

Lance Wenke slowly walked up to Mitch and said, "No hard feelings, Mitch, right? You know it was nothing personal."

"Don't kid yourself, Lance." Mitch said. "It doesn't get any more personal than this."

"Mitch, I was just doing my job."

"Sure, Lance," Mitch answered, "but you better update your resume, since you'll soon be doing it elsewhere."

Kari Landau, sitting behind her husband, reached out to him and they embraced, kissed, and embraced again.

"I love you, baby," she said.

"I love you too, sweetheart. Thank you for everything." Mitch said sincerely.

"Oh, don't worry, babe, I can think of plenty of ways for you to thank me." Kari said jokingly, breaking the severe tension that characterized their relationship for far too long.

In the back of the courtroom, Tess Lowe and Jack Tatum finally made their way through the crowd to reach each other. Tess spoke first.

"Detective, thank you so much for everything you have done. Listening to you on the stand gave me a sense of satisfaction and closure I so desperately needed."

"Ms. Lowe. It is I who need to thank you for saving my life." Jack said.

"Saving your life? I don't understand."

Jack reached into his jacket pocket and took out the business card case with the bullet hole in it. He stumbled as he handed it to Tess. His wife Kate, by his side, held him up by his elbow.

"I gave this to you at the station when . . ."

"Yes. The bullet went right through it, but the case diverted it so that it missed my heart. It, you, saved my life."

"I don't know what to say," Tess searched for words.

"You don't need to say anything, Tess," Kate spoke. "We will never forget this."

Six Weeks Later

In the lobby of the Siam Bank in Bangkok, the American tourist, Vincent Taylor, bearing an incredible resemblance to the fugitive from justice, George Stone, was conferring with his banker about the best way to move his money to another offshore account. Mr. Khanh seemed to take an unusually long time looking things up on his computer and taking phone calls from other customers. George was getting irritated. He had a million dollars in this bank, and certainly deserved to be treated better.

He came to terms with losing his house. It was a big loss, and he resented the way he was conned, although it was really his fault. There were plenty of red flags, and, in his rush to cash out, he chose to ignore them. On the other hand, George reasoned, if they did not take the house, it could have been seized, and he would have lost it that way. He had to make a quick decision, and there was no use blaming himself for making the best choice under the circumstances. Besides, on some level, he was impressed with the con. They were amateurs, but they were good. They conned a con man, and George was never one to think that there was room for only one of him in the world. He had plenty of money to keep going, time, and certainly the brains to make up the loss.

George learned about Bellinger's troubles from the internet, and even caught a CNN headline. It was not a frequent occurrence that a district attorney fell so hard and so deservedly. This was more than a local story. This was juicy. Landau won the election but, amazingly, not by a landslide. In its fervor to flavor punch a story, the press presented the case as one with remaining questions. Yes, Bellinger asked for evidence to be destroyed. Yes, he took illegal campaign contributions. Yes, he lied on the stand. But do we really know which one of them let the location of the critical state witness leak? It was a better story if it was not completely solved. Nonetheless, Bellinger was in jail and Landau was the new D.A. It certainly did not bode well for a prompt return to the United States.

Mr. Khanh stood up from his desk, and uneasily looked passed George.

"Mr. Stone." Asked an unfamiliar voice.

George rose to his feet and faced the man calling him by his real name.

"No. I am Vincent Taylor." He said.

"Sure you are," the man quipped. "You are also Walter Manning and, I am sure, a number of other names."

"I have no idea what you are talking about." George insisted.

"I see," the man continued. "Perhaps this will help you remember." The man motioned to a Thai police officer in uniform standing by the front door of the bank.

Charlie Parks, accompanied by another Thai police officer, walked into the bank and stopped at the front door.

"Is this the asshole?" The man called out to Charlie.

Charlie nodded.

"Is your memory jogged, Mr. Stone? By the way, we would have brought your pal, Grant Bellinger, here to greet you, but he is presently negotiating a deal with the new district attorney, Mitchell Landau, for that trivial charge of conspiracy to commit murder of a vital prosecution witness, Hsiao Tzu, although I wouldn't count on too much leniency from the new D.A. He doesn't take contributions from scumbag criminals like you. Turn around." The man ordered as he pushed Stone's face hard into the cold wood of the nearby desk, breaking his nose in the process.

"You killed my partner, you son of a bitch." Stanley Wolfson muttered as he handcuffed Stone and led him away.

Parker Center—The Following Monday

"Tess. It's great to see you again." Charlie said.

"You never quit, do you, Charlie. Dressed in prison garb and staring at six months in jail, you still think you can charm your way into anything." Tess replied.

"Hey, I helped you, didn't I? You've got all the money back and then some, and Stone's in jail."

"That's why I'm here. I know what you did you did for yourself. But, still, without you, it wouldn't have happened. So, I do thank you for that."

"You're welcome." Charlie meant it. "So, how about dinner when I get out?"

Tess shook her head.

"You'll never change. You should think about everything that happened. You should use this time wisely."

"Lunch then?"

"Good bye, Charlie." Tess said standing up and began walking out.

"Hey, Tess." Charlie called out. Tess stopped and looked back at Charlie, sitting there at a table in a room with other prisoners and their visitors. "Thanks."

"For what?" Tess asked.

"For not vilifying me. I was pretty rotten to you. But in truth, I really wasn't thinking. I just did what I always did for an easy buck. I did not set out to hurt you. But I know I did. And before you say it meant nothing, and you're not hurt, that's not the point. The point is that we were intimate and, with that, comes certain vulnerability. I should have never taken advantage of you that way, and I just wanted to say I'm sorry for that."

"Don't be too hard on yourself, Charlie. You gave us Reggie Blair and we got all of our money back."

"See, Tess, that's just it. Even that I did because I was pissed at George for not cutting me in on the sale of his house. I felt entitled to it. After all I did to you, to Jim Pane, to Milly, when the chips were down, I did not do what I did to help you. I did it for me. And the worst thing is, as much as I have tried over the past months to feel bad about it, I just don't. I can't get beyond thinking it's just money. But I do feel badly about you, and using you the way I did. I guess even I have boundaries."

"Take care of yourself, Charlie." Tess said as she walked outside of Parker Center where Tommy was waiting for her in the car.

"How did it go?" He asked.

"If you don't mind, Tommy, I'd rather not talk about it. Let's just leave here and leave this all behind."

"Sure." Tommy said starting the car. "But I sure hate to give up my colorful Saudi client."

"You know, I would have paid anything to have been a fly on the wall when you got the deed from Stone."

"For a man who's weaved such a complicated web of crime and deception, he sure seemed like a plain simple guy. He was not at all what I expected."

"Thank you, Tommy." Tess said.

"You don't need to thank me. I haven't felt this good about being a lawyer in a long time. And, to be honest, I really loved helping you."

"Hey, Tommy, I've been meaning to ask you. What the hell does Res Ipsa Loquitur mean anyway?" Tess asked.

"It's a Latin term lawyers use. It literally means 'The thing speaks for itself.' In other words, something is so clear that no other evidence is needed. You think Stone will look it up in the prison library?"

"How strange." Tess said thoughtfully. "If it weren't for this whole debacle, I would have never come to you, and you and I wouldn't be here, together."

"Yes, we would have," Tommy disagreed. "I would have begged you to take me back, anyway. That whole 'I need space' thing. That's just what a man says when he means the exact opposite. And I mean the exact opposite."

"So how will I know when you really mean that you need space?" Tess asked.

"When I die." Tommy answered and drove the car.

CHAPTER

Postscript: Ten Years Later

On his sixtieth birthday, Grant Bellinger died. He had been in prison for six years of his ten-year sentence. He made the deal that very day, in the chambers of Judge Betty Spencer. Wenke, although not his counsel per se, advised him against it. But Bellinger was done. There was no upside to a prolonged fight. The longer they looked, the more they would find. The sooner he started his term, the sooner he would get out. Ten years was fair, he knew that. After all, two people were dead. He would be a man and take his punishment.

But Bellinger underestimated prison. With the same clouded judgment that he made decisions during his last year as the district attorney and, for that matter, much of his career, he assumed that, in prison, just as in his office, he would go to the head of the class. He would be respected and, perhaps even revered, by the lower echelon of human beings.

His talents as a prosecutor could easily be utilized by the prisoners who needed legal help. He, Grant Bellinger, would be as invaluable in prison as he had been outside. He would hold court, so to speak, in the prison library, writing habeas corpus briefs, and helping death row inmates live longer. Maybe, they would even let him attend some of the hearings. After all, his input would be helpful to the court, and isn't that what really mattered.

But Bellinger was sadly mistaken. The unsavory characters who made up the names on the numerous search warrants approved by the district attorney, and who cluttered the arraignment calendars of the overworked Criminal Courts Building, had no use for the likes of old Bellinger. They mocked him routinely, tortured him occasionally, and worse, ostracized him. He spent his days alone, sometimes scared, sometimes bored, but always weak, reduced, in that karmic way, to a meaningless blob that he, during his life, had accused so many people of being.

The irony was not lost on Grant. Somewhere, a long time ago, he was idealistic and righteous. During his days as JAG in the marines and then as a prosecutor, thinking of nothing else but to be a part of making things better for others. But somewhere, in the many years that followed, in the many cases that did not go his way for what he believed were all the wrong reasons, in the elections that he simply had to win, whatever the cost, he morphed into the same type of parasite that he had vowed to quash when he took the oath after passing the bar.

And so, in his sixtieth year, he died in his cell, in his sleep. Not because his health failed him. Not because any foul play befell him. But because, deep in his soul, he knew that his entire life had been played out. That the choices he had made led him exactly where he belonged, and it was time to leave. There was, simply and definitively, nothing else to say.

～

After his dramatic testimony that day that nailed his boss, Timothy Newsome, Jr. vowed never to return to a courtroom. In some circles, he was a hero. In others, a weasel who did nothing more than save his own skin. Little Timmy knew that he was neither. He was just a man, surrounded all of his life by those who wanted to be more than that, who strived to surpass the unceremonious existence he longed for, free from guile and deceit as much as overachievement and glory. He had no checklist in life, things that he had to have, heights he had to reach.

But that day, when Kari Landau confronted Bellinger so directly and fearlessly, ready to give up so much for the cause that was so dear, Newsome saw a glimpse of passion for something other than professional achievement or coveted accolades or crisp uniforms. He saw a woman, armed with love, and speaking clean truth, unabated by thoughts of what was best, just what was right. It was then he decided that he would turn over the tape to the Landau team and agree to testify.

And, for the first time in his life, as he walked out the doors of that courtroom, amidst the havoc of the aftermath, barely noticed by anyone, he was content with what he wanted and what he did not want. As if, when he speared Bellinger with that verbal sword, when he gave up what he was told was right for what he knew was righteous, he conquered the memory of his father and the demeaning chapters of his childhood.

But his father was right about one thing. He did choose to be a campaign manager for all the right and the wrong reasons. Just as a boy, from a distance, watching his father brandish his power like a shiny weapon but, in fear, never wanting to hold that power himself, Newsome would watch those in power grab more of the same, remaining close enough to touch, but never wanting to hold. Being a campaign manager was the right choice if he wanted to live by those wrong reasons.

Freed from the unyielding grasp of his father's memory, Newsome walked out of that courtroom that day, and never looked back. Ten years later, in the beautiful Napa Valley, California, Newsome was strolling amidst the vineyards, and gently cradling each branch. It would be a good year.

Two rows to his right, his workers were distributing fertilizer to his brand new crop.

"Hey, guys, want some ice tea?" He yelled out to his staff.

"No, thanks, boss, we're good."

❧

Four hundred miles to the south, in Simi Valley, California, a truck pulled in for service into Toyota/Lexis Park, a franchise owned and operated by Charlie Parks. Sitting at his desk, Charlie was closing another deal. On his desk was a glass eagle, an accolade awarded him by Toyota's corporate leadership during one of those stuffy black tie events with mediocre food and cheap wine.

Charlie served his six months with ease. He schmoozed his way into favor with both the prisoners and the prison staff. He even had an affair with a female doctor who made rounds in the hospital ward where Charlie chose to work. And, in a weird way, Charlie was glad for his prison experience. He now knew and conquered what he feared, and it was not that bad.

When he got out of prison, Charlie looked up his old buddy, Joey Cancino. It had been many years. Charlie was somewhat surprised to learn that Joey was now a legitimate businessman with his own automobile franchise. Joey hired Charlie and, in that fitting mentor-to-protégé manner, passed on his business to him when he retired.

Charlie actually thought of the entire Oregon Project as a success. After all, he lived well and traveled for a while, met and made love to a beautiful woman, and, then, like a white knight coming to the rescue, helped his woman get back what was taken from her. It mattered little that he was a co-conspirator who committed a crime. What truly mattered is that it all ended well, and that, objectively and subjectively, he got away with it.

∽

It was one of the best days Steven Lowe could remember.

He was rather nervous about everything going well, the weather, the caterer, the band. But it was all coming together now. The cloud cover burnt off in the morning, and the sun was warming his big back yard. The caterer and her assistant were busy putting the finishing touches on the tables, covered with white linen tablecloths, candles, and other perfectly matching accoutrement. On a side table, a large white three-layer cake, was glistening with an inscription on top that read, "Happy Ten Year Anniversary." He picked virtually everything himself. He wanted it to be a perfect anniversary celebration for his little sister.

"They're here," yelled Josh, running into the back yard.

Steven walked into the house and welcomed Tess and Tommy, the guests of honor.

"Don't run too far away now," Tess yelled to her three children who followed her into the house, and immediately ran outside to see their cousin Josh.

"Don't worry, Sis," Steven said. "You know I've always wanted a house full of kids. Come on, I have a surprise for you."

Steven led Tess and Tommy into the backyard filled with people, and pointed to the couple standing by the heating lamp.

"Jack." Tess said. "How did you find him?"

"Palm Desert is a small town," Steven answered, pleased that his surprise had the desired effect.

Jack looked good. They had not seen each other or spoken after their last meeting in the courthouse, each assuming that to do otherwise would be an imposition. They updated each other on the last ten years in a matter of minutes. Jack and Kate's life was simple and peaceful. Tess and Tommy's lives were much the same as before, except that they were now happily intertwined.

"Jack, Kate, I would like you to meet our children." Tess said. "Kids, come here a minute, please." The children complied.

"This is Judy, the youngest, Kenny, and this is Jack, our oldest."

"Jack," Tess spoke to her son, "this is Jack, the man you were named after."

"Nice to meet you," said an eight year old Jack.

"Nice to meet you too," said his namesake, and then addressed himself to Tess, "I should be naming children after you," he said. "You save my life."

"If it were not for you, Stone would have never been arrested. You made sure he was tracked down. You pushed the Thai police." Tess said.

That Jack did. After the preliminary hearing, he and Stanley Wolfson spent their waking hours looking for George Stone. They started with Reggie Blair who gave up all he knew and cooperated fully. They had a general idea where Stone was hiding out, but it took international cooperation to pinpoint him at the right place at the right time. Mitch, the new D.A., Jack, and Stanley called in every favor they had with the U.S. attorney's office, with the IRS, and anyone else they could tag. And every day that Jack worked on what seemed at times was an impossible task, he always carried with him the gold business card holder that Tess Lowe gave to him that fateful day.

~

In a first-class seat of the Singapore Airlines flight, George Stone sipped a glass of wine and browsed the in-flight menu. He would have the chicken, the salad, and ice cream for dessert, he told the flight attendant. No, he did not want his own portable DVD. He wanted to sleep and not be disturbed until they landed.

Stone reached into his pocket and pulled out two prescription pain killer tablets and swallowed them. His back was acting up—the remnant of sleeping on a prison cot for ten years. He did his time, paid his debt to society, and there was no reason for bitterness.

Sometimes, even when you think everything through carefully, there are forces out of your control that will interfere with a perfect ending. That force, Stone was convinced, was Bellinger. Unlike Stone, Bellinger was not a meticulous planner, a master strategist. He got too greedy and went too far, paying the ultimate price. He should have stopped with removing Hsiao Tzu from the equation,

194

but he reached too far off the boat, and fell into the water. Stone followed him only because they were tied by one lifeline. If he had had a chance to cut it, George thought, he would have.

Besides, being the ultimate pragmatist, George calculated how many years he would have served in prison if he were convicted for everything he had done, for all the crimes he had committed. Ten years was a fraction, a small price to pay for the luxury of his life, the successes of his ventures. Like a bad driver who runs red lights routinely paying only one ticket, being caught that one time.

His prison cell was only five away from Bellinger. Stone watched his powerful friend wilt into insignificance, and, one morning, heard of his death. Despite the blame he placed on Grant for his predicament, he felt sorry for him. Victory in the game of life, to Stone, was the count at the end. Bellinger lost the game. Stone, on the other hand, was on his way to his new home.

Of course, he was not as wealthy as he was ten years ago. He was short a home in Bel Air and the $1.5 million he had stashed in the Siam Bank, which was seized by the government. But they did not know and could not know about the $5 million in other offshore accounts. After all, only a shortsighted crook would fail to diversify his plenty. He was far from shortsighted. As such, he would live out his days in comfort and luxury, surrounded by the spoils of his successes, and untroubled by his past. And so, in the game of life, in the world according to George Stone, he was victorious.

~

On the corner of Ocean Avenue and Wilshire Boulevard in Santa Monica, California, an office building stands, reflecting in its floor to ceiling windows, the Pacific Ocean and all that accompanies it. Taking the elevator to the penthouse suite, a young man in his twenties, dressed in a business suit, straightened his tie and checked his hair in the elevator mirror. As the elevator doors opened, the man walked into the lobby and announced himself to the receptionist.

"I am here to see Mr. Jackson Boyd. I have an appointment."

"May I tell Mr. Boyd your name?" The receptionist asked.

"Yes, I am Patrick Walsh. I have an interview with him, for that law clerk position. I am a bit early."

"Please have a seat," the receptionist said. "I will let Mr. Boyd know you are here."

Ten minutes later, Jackson Boyd walked into the lobby and introduced himself to the young man.

"Come with me," he said, leading the young Walsh into a large conference room at the end of the hallway, where Jackson's two partners were waiting for him. As he introduced them, Patrick sat down where he was directed, and took a deep breath.

"So," started Jackson, "why do you want to work for the law firm of Landau and Boyd."

Jackson Boyd, Mitchell Landau, and Kari Landau listened carefully as the young man explained how he had an intense interest in criminal law, the Constitution, and how, with all due respect to the defense law firm for which he was interviewing, he wanted, more than anything, to become a prosecutor, and hopefully, a district attorney.

"Then why aren't you applying for a clerkship with the D.A.'s office. I know they're hiring." Asked Mitch.

"Because, in my opinion, sir, one cannot be a good prosecutor unless one knows what it's like to be on the other side. I know I am young, and this may sound idealistic, but I believe that it is the role of both the prosecutor and the defense attorney to uphold the law, to uphold the rights of those rightly and wrongly accused."

The interview continued for twenty more minutes, with the three prospective employers asking questions. They liked the young man, and he would be offered the job, but there were others to interview, and, right now, they could only promise him that they would let him know by the end of the week.

When the interview was over, Patrick Walsh, hopeful, but uncertain about whether he got the job, decided to ask what was on his mind.

"Mr. Landau, may I ask you a question."

"Sure." Mitch responded.

"I've read about your election and the events surrounding it. And one thing kind of mystified me, maybe because I want to be where you were. Why, after such a struggle to get the office you had said in the press you had always wanted, you served only one term and resigned. You were, by all accounts, a hell of a D.A."

"Because some experiences in life shake your foundation, make you see things the way you never did. It's a bit hard to explain, Patrick. Perhaps if you get this job, we can talk more about it." Mitch said.

"I'd like that." Patrick answered as he walked out of the conference room.

In truth, it was not hard to explain at all. The first two years being the district attorney were, in short, unbelievably satisfying. Mitch was exactly where he wanted to be. He worked hard, made good changes, and made the right decisions. But then came the new campaign, the fundraising, the contributions and the expected promises in return. He was being challenged by one of his subordinates, a woman he respected and liked.

This was nothing compared to his battle with Bellinger, but the scent was rising. He could feel himself softening his once hard-line stances in order to appease, even slightly, those who would help him get reelected. He was breaking no laws, and crossing no lines. But he felt himself slipping into the Bellinger abyss, tasting, and for the first time, understanding what must have turned Bellinger from a good prosecutor into a corrupt politician.

In a good system of laws, this was a bad system of politics. In order to stay in power to do good, one had to succumb to allowing some bad. Nor did he see a good solution to this quagmire, although he contemplated it often. If, instead, the district attorneys were appointed for life, the way U.S. Supreme Court justices were, there would be no accountability other than one's own conscience, a rather weak monitoring system. And so, at the end of his term, Mitchell Landau resigned, without fanfare and with conscience in tact.

He and Kari would pursue what they talked about so many times. They would be partners doing criminal defense work. When Jackson heard about the plans, he could think of no better partners. There was the playful exchange about whose name would go first on the firm's logo. Over dinner, they did everything from drawing slips of paper out of a hat to flipping a coin. Jackson did make the lackluster argument that his name came first alphabetically. Finally, it was decided that Landau and Boyd was simply easier to pronounce than Boyd and Landau, and, after all, there were two Landaus and only one Boyd.

At times, Mitchell got questioned about his switch from putting away criminals to defending them. But he would answer that the question assumed facts not in evidence.

"They are not all criminals. They are not all guilty. And while my shingle welcomes equally the guilty and the innocent, who are both entitled to the best defense, it is the wrongly accused I long to represent, that innocent person I aim to serve."

About the Author

Natasha Roit was born in the Soviet Union and immigrated to the US when she was fourteen years old. She earned the prestigious Clay Award, which named her the California Trial Lawyer of the Year in 2003, and in 2004 was named one of the top fifty female attorneys by the *Daily Journal*. She represented the Browns against O. J. Simpson in the custody battle for Sydney and Justin Simpson and won on appeal. Her accomplishments in the courtroom are legend and have earned her and her clients record financial settlements. She graduated from Loyola Law School in Los Angeles and won a graduate fellowship to study the Chinese language and culture after completing her B.A. at UCLA. She is a sought after speaker at various trial lawyer symposiums and conventions. She lives in Malibu, California. This is her debut novel and she is already hard at work on her second mystery thriller.